AN AVALON WESTERN

TAYSHAS
Joe Burkett

Tired and dusty from the trail back east, Tom Cooper stops in a Texas saloon for a quiet drink. When a loud-mouthed drunk challenges him, the gun play results in the stranger's death and the sheriff advises Cooper to leave quickly. The dead man's family, the Landis's, who are the local bullies, set after him.

While fleeing the Landis gang, Cooper is attacked by a giant black panther, but manages to escape the ferocious beast. Eventually, he stumbles on the land of Shane and Martha Peters. They help the injured man and a bond is formed between Cooper and their daughter, Belle. Cooper finds peace with the Peters family and friendship or "taysha" with their Hasinai Caddo neighbor, Sam Waters. However, the Landis gang discover his whereabouts and they are determined to kill anyone who gets in their way. Will they succeed in their deadly mission?

TAYSHAS

•

Joe Burkett

AVALON BOOKS
NEW YORK

PRINTED IN THE UNITED STATES OF AMERICA
ON ACID-FREE PAPER
BY HADDON CRAFTSMEN, BLOOMSBURG, PENNSYLVANIA

To my grandmother, Leona Harrison Burkett,
who gave me my first western book to read which
inspired me to become a western writer.

Chapter One

The rain turned to sleet and came down slowly, landing on the brim of his brown, felt hat and the shoulders of his duster. It glistened softly on the mane of the coal-black mustang. All was quiet except for the horse's hooves plodding on the frozen earth.

Tom Cooper was a sandy-haired man of medium height, not too heavy but nonetheless powerful. He was the type very likely to be overlooked in a crowd as nothing exceptional. The north wind blew cold and hard through the trees, and it made him appreciate his beard and gloves.

He had been riding to Texas for four days after quitting his job at a horse ranch in eastern Louisiana. Originally from Ohio, he'd come south after fighting the Confederates in what had been dubbed the Civil War.

1

He still remembered well when his brother and best friend fell at the siege of Mobile, Alabama. That day was burned into his brain, and there had been nothing civil about it.

With no one left for him to come home to, he had hoped to make a new life for himself. Tom had since accumulated a small stake by working on the ranch and doing odd jobs. But so far, he'd had no real success, for the South was still trying to reconstruct.

It was late evening, and the sky was a dark lead color. The sleet finally stopped, yet both the man and the animal's breath made little clouds of fog in the air.

Cooper loved to ride and enjoyed taking the back trails. From directions he'd received at a few homesteads, he knew that he couldn't be very far from Bentosa, a little town only a short distance from the Sabine River. It was mostly a farming town with varying sizes of plantations still in operation and a few people around who raised cattle and hogs. However, those operations weren't large enough to be considered ranches.

Tom found a good place to camp and decided to stop for the night. It was a knoll with a grove of white oaks and maples. Considering the wet weather, the area was relatively dry. Another fitting campsite might not be found before dark, and there was no hurry. The trip could be resumed the next morning.

After the gelding was readied for the night, Tom soon built a crackling fire and had coffee boiling. It and jerked beef constituted his last meal of the day.

Tom's thoughts roamed to Texas. He was anxious to see the country and wanted a place of his own there. Things were getting too crowded in the East to suit him. As soon as he found a place that felt right, he would stay. God knew he had been in his share of unfriendly and unsuitable spots. Finally, he went to sleep with those thoughts in mind and the lonely howl of a wolf in his ears.

The chirping of sparrows high in the treetops overhead brought Cooper to wakefulness. Light was still faint, but he was eager to be moving. And so was the mustang. When Tom touched spurs to the animal it pranced a couple of yards before taking off at a lope.

A little more than an hour of riding brought him to a crude wagon road. It branched off into several dim trails and ran past a good number of farmhouses and cabins. Smoke curled upwards in the sunlight from every chimney.

Bentosa spread out ahead of him a little before noon. It consisted of only two building-lined streets that intersected in the center of town. Cooper drew rein in front of the first saloon. A drink would help warm him.

He tethered the black to the hitching rail and slipped the thong off the hammer of his Colt Army .44. The latter came natural even though he had never hunted trouble. Six rough-looking men seated at a far table instantly caught his eye upon entering. There were no other occupants save himself and the portly barman, probably because it wasn't quite noon. Tom only gave them a glance before stepping up to the counter, yet he figured he knew the type.

"Give me a whiskey," he said.

The short, dumpy bartender filled the order while Tom watched the men at the table in the mirror that stretched behind the bar. They were laughing and talking about everything and nothing in particular. One could easily tell that they had soaked up plenty from the two whiskey bottles that sat before them, despite the early hour. Cooper was glad that he had never been that crazy over liquor. He took a small sip from his own glass.

"Don't think I've seen you in here before," the bartender said pleasantly. "Where you hail from? Don't talk like anybody 'round these parts."

Staring down at the amber liquid, Cooper replied, "Ohio originally." That answer had changed attitudes toward him before. Maybe he just imagined that the six men's discussion lowered. "Came down a couple years back," he added. "Been living over close to the Mississippi little over a year."

Surprisingly, the man's smile never wavered. They talked for a few minutes about the soggy weather and the local happenings. Tom asked in a hushed tone about the rowdy group across the room when the conversation slowed.

The barman wiped his hands on his once white apron and leaned on the bar to whisper, "The Landis clan. They own a good little place about seven miles south of here. They used to have a a group of negroes that did the work, but it's went down since that was all stopped." There wasn't any anger in his voice like other Southerners Tom had heard speak of the freeing of Negroes.

Cooper took a drink. "Kind of loud, aren't they?"

"Meanest bunch you ever laid eyes on." The bar-keeper grunted and shrugged his shoulders. "Saloon owner's gotta put up with a lot to make a profit. The sheriff don't take none of their foolishness, though."

Tom nodded to himself; he had pegged them for bullies. He finished his whiskey but lingered at the bar, rolling a smoke. The warm room and conversation felt relaxing after being out in the elements for so long a time. He didn't take any more notice to the lowered speech of the Landises, nor did he see the hard looks they cast at his back.

The saloon proprietor was telling more about the town troublemakers. "That big, proud lookin' one is Ike. Oldest and ramrods the bunch. He rides that big bay out front."

There was plenty more riding to do and Tom was getting ready to leave. He dropped the half-smoked cigarette into a clay ashtray and glanced in the mirror once again. "Who's that one on his left with the scarred face?"

"Bill, cousin to the rest. But they treat him like a brother." One by one, he told the others names.

Suddenly a chair slid across the floor and a smug voice queried, "Hey Yankee, you care to share what y'all are mumblin' about with the rest of us?"

The barman glanced warily at Tom and stepped back away from the counter. Cooper looked into the mirror and saw the youngest of the men standing a little way from the table. His face was flushed red by liquor, and, like the others, a pistol adorned his lean hips, arm hanging close by.

Tom wanted to curse. They had indeed heard him say he was from Ohio. He turned away from the bar and averted, "Just shootin' the bull."

A dark, curly-haired man reached up and grasped his younger brother's arm. "Randy, sit down!"

Randy jerked away and returned hotly, "Leave me be, Dirk!" With his attention once again focused on Tom, he declared, "I say you was talkin' about us."

"No, Son, we weren't." Cooper read all six as fighting men, and he didn't like where things were headed. A lot of trouble might be avoided by lying.

"I ain't a liar. My brothers fought you dirty bastards in the war."

"That's in the past," the barkeeper said from behind Tom. "Besides, you don't even know if this fella served."

Cooper managed to conceal his anger. This was just a young hothead filled up on redeye. But why didn't one of the others take charge of him?

Ike looked at the Northerner then to the dumpy barman. "We spend more money in here than this stranger passin' through, Ed." His whiskey-hazed brain flashed with scenes of carnage he'd seen on the battlefields.

"You'd best sit back down," Tom Cooper told Randy calmly.

The young man sneered. "Ain't no man gonna tell me what to do. Especially a damned Yankee."

Cal, the next in age to Randy, had his back to Tom and shifted in his chair to better see both factions. Short, stout James Landis said sternly, "Ease up, Randy. Let it ride!"

Ike wanted to see this Yankee tuck his tail. "Leave him alone, James. There's six of us. This guy's buckin' a stacked deck."

Still holding his temper somewhat in check, Cooper heard the truth in Ike's words, yet he kept his eyes riveted on the younger man. It was time to be moving and he should leave. But their arrogance got to him. "There shouldn't be trouble here," he said. "I was only giving some advice."

Randy Landis was confident. "Listen to this y'all, he's givin' me some advice." His eyes narrowed. "Now I'll give you some. You'd best get the hell out of here! If ya want to see the sun set, that is."

A man stepped through the swinging doors and, at the sight of the two facing one another, quickly decided to exit. Cooper saw this from the corner of his eye as he stepped away from the bar. He could no longer hold back, and his voice rose. "This is a drinking establishment and I got good money. And I'll be damned if some kid's going to tell me where I can and can't drink. Especially a damned Rebel!"

Bill suddenly disliked the stranger's hard look. There was something about it, and he moved to stop Randy. But it was too late as the latter cursed and reached for his gun.

Tom's right hand flashed to the Colt. The weapon came level and fired just as his opponent's cleared leather. The slug hit within the outline of Randy's shirt pocket, knocking him backwards to the plank floor.

Cal Landis's lithe body sprang from the chair to land kneeling beside his fallen brother. Ike and Bill stood and went for their guns, chairs clattering to the floor. Then they suddenly stopped. Dirk and James were in half-standing positions when they halted.

The Colt Army was at arm's length in Tom's hand, fully cocked and trained on Ike's forehead. Yet he didn't believe they had stopped their play solely because of that. All were looking past him. He took a furtive look over his shoulder and saw, to his amazement, Ed holding a sawed-off, double-barreled shotgun with hammers eared back.

"I don't think y'all want to continue this nonsense," the barkeeper speculated. "I'm sure this fella can get one more of ya, and I can put at least two of ya outta commission with this here scattergun."

Twisting around on his knees, Cal cried, "Randy's dead! He killed him!"

The other family members moved their hands away from their sidearms and went over to him. Cooper lowered the hammer on his six-gun and slid it back into its holster. Ed laid the greener in easy reach on the bar. Neither man removed his gaze from the group.

There was the pounding of boots outside on the boardwalk, then a bearded man with a silver star pinned to his vest and a pistol in hand charged through the batwing doors. He instantly looked to the bartender after seeing the Landises clustered around the body. "Ed, what happened in here?"

Cal stood up, pointed an accusing finger at Tom, and bellowed, "I'll tell you what happened! He killed Randy!"

"That may be so, Sheriff, but Randy drew first. Instigated the whole mess. Just look, there's his gun lying next to him." Ed defended Tom.

The Landis clan stood there looking sad and solemn, sobered by the sudden events. Ike's clouded mind had figured wrong. This stranger hadn't backed away from the odds and now Randy was gone, the youngest of them gunned down before his life had gotten a good start.

Ike felt a true hatred for this man he'd just met. He had fought those Federals, and killed his share of them too.

To think that one of them had killed his little brother, who hadn't even been old enough to fight in the war, made him swell with fury. He wouldn't admit that he was wrong.

"What have you got to say?" the sheriff inquired, staring at Cooper. The lawman's pistol still hung loosely in his hand.

Tom's anger had subsided, yet his voice was tense. He only wanted to be away from here. "The kid, Randy, was butting into my conversation. Tried to run me off. He was plenty drunk and we argued some. Then he drew on me. After I shot him, these others started to grab iron. If it weren't for the barkeep and his scattergun, I'd be dead right now."

"He's a damn liar!" Cal Landis exclaimed.

The bearded man with the star glared hard at the

Landises for a long moment, then turned to the bar and said, "You've always run a decent place here, Ed. And I know you'd never lie to protect a cold-blooded murderer. I also know the reputation of these boys." He turned to the Landises and silenced an outburst of oaths from Ike with an uplifted hand. "Y'all have a tendency to get drunk, and a few of you have been in my jail before.

"Now I'm sorry about Randy. But seeing as his gun was drawn, and Ed and this fella's stories agree, and since there aren't any more witnesses, I don't see any reason to arrest him. Couldn't hold him very long if I did."

After the lawman finished his speech, Cal, in his same loud voice, blurted, "Dang it all," then rushed outside.

Ike pointed a warning finger at Tom. "I got business to tend to. But just because the law won't do nothing about this don't mean we won't. We'll come lookin' for you. I'll hunt you down like a mangy cur."

"That'll be enough!" The sheriff meant what he said. "Now go get the undertaker."

Tom Cooper could almost feel Ike's menace pierce his skin. The rest of the Landises silently followed the big man out. Only Bill gave him another enraged look. A shiver threatened Tom as he watched them go.

"What's your name, Mister?" the sheriff asked.

"Thomas Cooper. I go by Tom, though."

Ike Landis paused just outside the doors long enough to hear the reply.

The sheriff was sympathetic, but advised, "Well,

Cooper, it'd be a good idea if you left town. They won't forget this."

Tom glanced to Ed. "So I've heard. I do need to get some things at the mercantile, first."

"All right, but as quickly as possible." Bentosa's sheriff holstered his gun and departed as quickly as he'd appeared.

Cooper's mind was spinning as he replaced the spent cartridge in his own revolver. He reached into his pocket and flipped three silver dollars onto the bar.

Ed frowned. "That's way too much, Cooper."

"It's not only for the whiskey. It's for backing up a stranger. Obliged," he asserted and walked out, leaving the bartender and bloody corpse behind.

Chapter Two

The air outside chilled Cooper after being in the warmth of the barroom. He stood on the desolate boardwalk, looking up and down the street. It was deserted except for a few people going about their daily tasks. The sawmill at the edge of town was the busiest building in sight. There were none of the Landises anywhere that he could see, so he ambled north, staying close to the wall.

A potbellied stove warmed the general store, and two old men sat nearby, reliving times past and telling yarns. Tom passed bolts of calico and other materials to examine some clothing. He listened faintly to the old-timers discuss the earlier gunfire while he selected a good poncho, shirt and pair of pants, jerked beef, quite a bit of cigarette makings, a small amount of flour, coffee, and salt, along with some matches. He placed the items on the counter next to several jars of candy.

"You must be making a long trip," predicted the slim clerk after adjusting his tiny spectacles.

"Headed to Texas. Not sure how far, yet," Tom remarked. "Put a box of .44's and a box of .56's on the bill, too."

He was careful not to arouse suspicion but hurried the merchandise back to his waiting mustang after paying for it. With the saddlebags carefully packed and a supply of tobacco, rolling papers, and matches in his shirt pocket, Cooper stepped into the saddle and headed the black toward the west side of town.

Ike, Bill, and Cal Landis came out of an alley. Anger burned in all three as they watched the Northerner leave. Ike had an almost uncontrollable urge to put a slug into the man's back. But he knew it would be a foolhardy move at present. The sheriff wasn't stupid; he would know who had done it.

Instead, Ike spat and drawled, "We'll get him!"

Tom Cooper had ridden about five miles when rain started to fall. It came slowly at first, then finally in sheets, streaming off his hat and new poncho. This, he decided, was the worst rain he had been in since beginning his westward trek.

The ground was soggy, and finding a dry place to camp would be difficult. Yet what really worried him was the distance that still lay between him and the Sabine. Crossing on a ferry would be a lot less risky, although that would mean sticking to the road. But remembering the cold look of Ike Landis, Tom preferred the back trails to the more traveled routes.

His mind wandered to the man he had killed. Actually, he'd just been a cocky kid, trying to prove himself with a gun. Many a young man had died the same way, and no doubt a lot of premature deaths were still to come. Guilt settled on him as it does anyone who has ever taken a human life. Yet what else could he have done?

He shook his head; he could have left like they wanted him to. Darn it, that wasn't right either. What gave them the right to dictate where he or any other man drank? Still, it would have saved trouble and a life.

Randy Landis made the fourth man to fall under his hand since the war. In Alabama one man went down from a knife in a barroom fight that originated over a woman. Two bandits died by his gun when they tried to rob him as he passed through Mississippi. In all cases it was self-defense, but now he vowed to himself that if there was any way to avert more trouble, he would do it. Tom was tired of the fighting. He'd had a gut full of that during the war.

Darkness came sooner than usual due to the bleak sky. A dense growth of post oaks and pines provided a somewhat pleasant encampment. Cooper slipped the bit from the gelding's mouth but, though he loosened the cinch a little, he left the saddle on, partly for the horse's warmth, and partly so he could ride quickly if the Landises showed. He told himself that was unlikely as he searched for something to build a fire with. The rain had subsided, but a half-hour was spent in locating only wet wood.

He uttered a curse at remembering his canteen was empty. At least it wasn't hot weather, and he could make do without water for one night. There was likely a branch or creek that he would come to the next day. If not, the river wasn't far away. He wasn't in the mood for much of a meal, anyway.

The wind gusted and made him shiver. After a last cigarette, he spread his blankets behind a windbreak of yaupons. With the poncho placed over him in case of more rain, he closed his eyes, hand gripping the Colt. His miserableness and worry made sleep fitful.

The Landis brothers were grouped around the big kitchen table. Bill was also there, amid the yellow lamplight.

"Well, I'm darn sure goin' after him," Ike declared. "I know Cal's goin' with me. Who else is?"

Dirk looked at each of the two. "Y'all both know good'n well that Randy started it. If you go after that man, you'll get yourselves killed. That fella was mighty good with that six-shooter! Better than most."

"I say you're yellow and ain't got no family pride," Ike said, and Cal nodded in agreement to his older brother's words.

Dirk was mad now. "You know I can outshoot any of you!"

"This may be true," Ike conceded. "But do you have the guts to go against somebody just as good?"

There was a tense moment of silence in which Dirk was forming a reply. He didn't like going off half-cocked. Bill spoke before he did. "I'll go, Ike. After all, I helped raise Randy."

"Thanks. Ain't none of us married, so we don't have nothing holding us back," Ike concluded. "We shouldn't be gone long and the place will be fine." His questioning gaze was fixed on Dirk.

Thoughts flew through James's mind. He'd always been cautious and liked to think things through. "I'm in. But we sure as hell better have a plan. Because if we just go in on him a-shootin', some of us will get our guts blown out."

"That makes four of us," Cal said. He looked at Dirk. "What's another dead carpetbagger, anyhow? They all got a lot of gall comin' down here!"

Dirk shook his head in disgust, then banged the tabletop with his fist, nearly upsetting the lamp. "All right! Like James said, though, we need a plan to keep from gettin' shot to hell."

"That'll come later. Right now I just want to blow his brains out," Ike stated flatly. "Soon as Randy's buried in the morning, we'll ask the fella runnin' that store if Cooper might have said where he was headed. It'll be hard to hit a trail with all this rain. He might not have taken the roads." As the others stood and prepared to retire for the night, Ike smiled to himself and murmured, "But we'll get him eventually." Once again he had convinced his family to see things his way.

*   *   *

Tom was tightening the cinch when the first rays of sunlight filtered through the heavy pine and oak timber. It hadn't rained any more during the night, and he hoped the river wasn't too bad. However, he would soon find out.

He noticed as he rode that the terrain was getting much thicker with undergrowth. There had been stands of open timber before. Now, dense thickets of yaupons, myrtles, and laurels clogged the way and made him wonder if traveling the wagon roads might not have been wiser.

His theory of being close to a creek was proven correct upon coming to one a couple of miles further on. The waterway ran level with its banks and was some twelve feet wide. Tom presumed it to be about four feet at the deepest as he knelt and filled his canteen with the murky water. He let the mustang drink while arranging his gear.

As he crossed the creek his saddlebags hung over his left shoulder to keep their contents dry. With both the Spencer carbine and reins in his right hand, Cooper urged the black ahead. At the midpoint, the ice-cold water poured into his boots.

Although Tom didn't get wet above the knees, the chilly air made his leg muscles taught as the animal brought him smoothly out on the opposite side. His feet were numb with cold, and he stepped down long enough to pour the water from his boots and place the gear back in its original position.

He had heard about the wide open spaces out West and wished that he was there so he could ride faster.

The brush hindered progress greatly, and sometimes he had to take a detour before continuing toward Texas. A hot meal and fire would have been great, but he was determined to put the Sabine behind him first.

Cane soon added to the variety of undergrowth, and he saw plenty sign of game. Another hour passed before he came to a halt on the muddy bank of the Sabine River. The waterway, which made up part of the Louisiana-Texas border, was swollen into a dangerously swift current.

Looking out over the river, Tom thought again of how much safer a ferry would be. "It's going to be rough, old boy."

He took the poncho and wrapped his extra clothes and bedroll in it before tying the bundle behind the cantle. Maybe it would help some. The .56 Spencer was held this time on his left shoulder along with the saddlebags. Since the horse would have to swim, he wanted his right hand to be free.

Soon they were in the swirling water. After going several feet, the current lifted the mount's hooves off bottom. Cooper held tightly, trying not to slip from the saddle while the horse labored to keep afloat. It was all he could do to keep the rifle and saddlebags above water. Maybe he should have left the former in the boot. Now, because he was trying to keep the weapon dry, where it wouldn't have to be so thoroughly cleaned, he might lose it in the river. Already his muscles felt numb, and he wondered about the gelding's own strength.

The struggling team of man and animal had been

pushed thirty yards downstream and were not even halfway across when the horse swayed to the left, causing Cooper to begin sliding from the saddle. His legs seemed not to respond when his brain told them to tighten around the horse. He grasped the pommel and managed to right himself with a mighty heave.

Clothing drenched, he clung to the saddlebags, carbine, and most importantly, the saddle. They were nearly across and the mustang had stamina. "C'mon boy. We'll make it," Tom encouraged.

The gelding's feet finally made contact with the bottom and brought them lurching and splashing out onto the bank. Both were drenched and very cold. The Colt and cartridges that were in his gunbelt had been completely under water. But the pistol would be easier cleaned than the Spencer, and hopefully the metal cartridges would save the powder, as they were made to.

Tom knew his mount was tired, probably more so than himself. He murmured a prayer of thanks and urged the animal on about two hundred and fifty yards into the junglelike growth that ran along the river before coming to a small, rather open grove of red oaks. It would make a good camp and Cooper hurried to prepare one. A thicket of pine saplings and yaupons grew on the northern edge, making a much needed windbreak.

With teeth chattering, Tom donned a pair of older clothes from his pack. The poncho had kept the things relatively dry, and against his icy skin the shirt and pants felt wonderful. He hung his others, along with the duster and long johns, on some branches to dry.

While sitting close to a small fire he'd built, he wiped the revolver down with a soft cloth. He always took care of his weapons; that was something he learned from his Army experience. The cartridges from his gunbelt were scattered over his blankets to rid all the water from them.

Tom wanted to make sure they would fire, so he filled the cylinder of the Army Colt and eared back the hammer. He aimed the gun at a young pine and slowly squeezed the trigger. Flame and noise erupted from the muzzle, and the tree was almost snapped in two by the heavy slug. Behind him the mustang shied, and Tom spoke a soothing word while replacing the spent round.

He had tried to keep his thoughts off Randy Landis, but now he stared at the gun in his hand and reflected on its life-taking power. After a while, he built up the fire with the amount of dry wood he had found in the brush. His horse stood close by, absorbing the warmth, too.

The day was waning, and he finally became warm, the muscle cramps subsiding. Eating jerky was getting tiresome, so he slipped into the duster, which he considered dry enough to wear, picked up the carbine, and started back toward the river in search of game. He turned south after covering half the distance.

It was rough going. Standing water had to be detoured in several places. Then a sea of thick cane and bunches of brown grass were all around him, except for an occasional water-loving tree. Further on, the former dispersed and he came onto a ridge with stands of white oaks and pin oaks. He gazed around and proceeded cautiously. This was a likely place for many types of game.

So this is East Texas, he mused. *Not all that different from Louisiana.*

The sky's grayness made the light disappear quicker. Yet the weather had been the usual for the past week, and Tom was used to the ominous heavens. At the knoll's crest he came to a halt, scanning the slushy baygall below. It looked as if beef jerky would be his supper after all.

Just as he was about to turn, a terrific weight hit Tom in the upper back and a sharp pain dug into his flesh. He went down, lunging sideways and dropping the rifle in the fall. Cooper landed on his right shoulder, rolled, and returned to his feet, every nerve on end and ready for action.

Chapter Three

A dark blur slammed into his chest and knocked him flat on his back. Again there was a slicing pain, this time on the inner part of his thighs and chest.

Pushing and kicking at the giant panther, Tom looked up to see the bright, yellow eyes and long, white teeth, which he knew were capable of tearing a man's throat out. The animal's front paws were seized on Cooper's shoulders while the claws on its hind feet were slashing to disembowel him. Only Tom's constantly moving legs and twisting body prevented the latter. He could smell the animal's breath and feel the warm stickiness of his own blood running into his clothes. True fear was upon him.

He somehow managed to fling the big cat away, kicking it back with his boot. Before Tom could rise,

22

the panther wheeled for another attack. It was met by the smashing of his boot again, and he reached frantically for his .44. The beast had crouched and was in midair when the gun roared. The panther's head jerked under the impact and its body fell twitching in Cooper's lap.

He tried to slow his breathing and pushed the cat aside. At a glance to the huge pin oak limbs above him, Tom knew he'd been standing almost directly under the cat. His pants were slashed much worse than his shirt, but the dark wet patches on both were enough to cause significant worry.

It was almost dark when he made it back to camp, and he quickly undressed to assess the damage by the dim light of the dying fire. There were several cuts on his chest and shoulders, yet the deepest were on the upper part of his legs. The claws had sliced furrows up to five inches long and all were bleeding freely. He couldn't tell much about the ones on his back but figured they were at least as bad as those on his chest.

Although there were several short tears on the back of the duster, there was only a small amount of blood on the inside, which made him feel better about them. Likely, they would have been worse if he hadn't reacted so fast.

Tom Cooper raked some ashes from the fire and, after they had cooled, packed all of the cuts he could reach with them. The flow of blood was soon stanched. Yet the raw flesh showed its tenderness as he dressed in the outfit he'd crossed the river in and made some coffee and biscuits to have with the dried beef.

Cooper leaned back against his saddle and rolled a cigarette when the meal was over, trying to relax his already sore muscles. What else would happen? The Landises popped into his mind once again.

Upon first laying eyes on them it was easy enough to see that they were a rough lot. The bartender's words and their own actions had assured the fact. Maybe they would come after him, but he comforted himself with the fact that he had seen no sign of them as of yet.

Luck, Tom knew, had been with him during the panther attack. His wounds could have been much worse, even fatal, but he ought to rest and make sure they would heal, just for a day or two. Cat claws were none too clean, and infection was always a danger. Although, if he did sit around, it would surely give Ike and the others time to catch up, supposing they were coming. And the notion of fighting five men while he was hurt wasn't appealing.

Thumping the cigarette into the glowing embers of the fire, he slipped between the blankets. Right now he needed sleep, he could decide in the morning.

The Landis men were camped a few miles east of the Sabine. The clerk at the mercantile had unknowingly helped their malicious intent by relating where Cooper was headed.

Ike was squatted by the fire he'd just built. He was a little concerned at the scant tracks they had found.

It had taken them until noon to find the trail of their prey.

"What with all the darn rain we've had, it's hard to read sign a day old," he remarked.

Dirk had been sullen most of the day. The sight of Randy's coffin being lowered into that hole right after daylight still lingered in his mind. "I can't believe we're makin' this trip. Ain't got no right lookin' for trouble with this man."

"Well, I say we do! But if you want to back out, go right ahead," Ike said sarcastically.

There was no response save the shaking of Dirk's head. James quickly said, "It ain't rained in awhile, so maybe it'll be easier tomorrow. Most of his sign was washed out by that shower after he left."

Ike Landis lay for a long time that night thinking of the man that shot his kid brother. That he'd been there and not able to stop it, ate at him. Though maybe he could have. He had expected the Yankee to slink away at the odds. There was no look about Cooper that said he was a gunslick, but now Ike could only see the flash of the stranger's gun and Randy falling back. Ike clenched his teeth and eyes in an attempt to stop the visions.

What really got to him was that Randy hadn't been subjected to the slaughter of the war because of his age, then, at only nineteen, he was killed by a Yankee. Ike hated this man more than any he had ever known. Yes, he would see him die. Then Randy's death would be avenged.

* * *

Tom awoke just as the first light of day came flickering through the trees. The sky was surprisingly clear. His body protested but he began preparations to move on.

It took almost an hour for him to have things ready. With his bloody, tattered clothing in hand, he rode back to the river. They were ruined and he didn't want to leave them where his pursuers—if indeed there were any—might find them. He sat the black and watched the current swirl the clothes away, glad that his long johns hadn't been on his person during the fight with the panther.

He enjoyed riding through the rich river bottom and continuously altered his course. At that early hour he saw many squirrels and rabbits and even a couple of deer. A flock of robins flew up into the tops of a stand of black gums at his sudden intrusion on their hunt for breakfast. There seemed to be plenty of game, and Cooper wished he would have seen such the evening before.

The surroundings were tranquil as he wound slowly through the thickets and timber. Sometime around noon, he ate the leftover biscuits and more jerky while traveling.

He wasn't sure of what kind of work he could get, but maybe he could find something working with horses. After all, that was what he liked and knew most about.

By late afternoon he came to a dim road. Turning sharply, he followed it northwest. Only once had he come close to any sign of habitation, the back of a field that was overgrown with weeds and shrubs, which he'd given a wide berth. The zigzagging trail he left was meant for any followers, however some of the apprehension that filled him the day before was now gone. Whiskey and anger could make men say a lot.

The sun was once again hidden by dark clouds that threatened more rain. Tree branches arched over the wagon road from both sides, intertwining overhead. It cast a foreboding feeling, and Cooper sighed.

The killing was all supposed to be over with upon the surrender of General Lee. Tom still felt badly over the incident, as he did many others in his life, but some of the guilt had left him because he was sure Randy would have killed him. No one drew on an armed man without that intention. It would be crazy.

Being a Northerner was why he sparked so much hatred in them. He had seen plenty of it since coming south. Almost five years had passed since the last battle, yet it was hard for people to forget what had happened to their friends and families. He understood all this. He himself had even harbored bad feelings for the South right afterwards. It was natural. And the Union had done a great deal of damage to the Confederate States; they were still recovering.

Tom Cooper was brought out of his contemplation by the spattering of rain on his hat brim. Reaching behind him, he got the poncho and draped it over his shoulders. The loneliness of the trail strained at his nerves, and seeing the late hour, he shucked the Spencer from its scabbard. Partly because of what had taken place the night before—though it was highly unlikely to happen again—and because he still wanted some fresh meat.

The carbine roared a half-mile further on, the slug felling a young cottontail. Tom, knowing that the game would be easier dressed while it was still warm with body heat, quickly swung off into the seclusion of the timber and, with the rain stopped, made camp. He soon had the preparations for the meal underway.

When the biscuits were finally done, he sat down to what seemed a feast after so many days of jerky. As long as there is game around, I won't starve, he thought with a mouth full of the roasted meat.

The aching of his wounds made him undress to clean them again after the meal. They were jagged red lines in his flesh, extremely tender to the touch. But they didn't show signs of infection. Tom estimated it to be right at the freezing mark, and he was more than glad to get back into his clothes.

As the light faded, there was the hint of snow in the air, or so he thought. From what experience he had and what he'd heard, there wasn't any great amount of that kind of precipitation in these parts. However, there had been occasional times when drifts of two or three feet were seen. Hopefully this wouldn't be one of those occasions.

Lying in his blankets, Cooper wondered about the type of people he would encounter here in Texas. Were they more or less the same as the ones in Louisiana? Would most be against him? It was doubtless some would; there were good and bad people every-

where. Yet he did know that Texas hadn't been rav-
aged like other parts of the South. Mostly they had
helped by sending men, food, and supplies east.

Cooper gradually began to doze, actually hoping to
see some civilization the next day. Although he had
been moving the entire day, he figured only around
four miles lay between him and his last camp. While
he had ridden much further, his winding route south
then back north hadn't taken him very far from the
Sabine.

The Landises found where Cooper had crossed the
river, and Ike decided to ford the flowing border a few
hundred yards upstream. Tom's camp was located, and
after a search, they started on the trail leading south.
Sign looked promising for a while, but it soon became
harder to read, and that, compounded with the cold,
damp weather, purpose of the journey, and sadness
over the loss of their sibling and cousin made them a
sour bunch.

Cal was next in age to Randy, and even though he
had seen a couple of men die violent deaths, the sight
of his brother lying on that sawdust-covered floor kept
running through his head, haunting him every mile of
the trip. He'd listened to stories about the war from
Ike and the others, yet he had no fighting experience
other than fisticuffs. Cal stayed home with their ma
and pa during the years of fighting to help with the
place and Randy. Many times, though, he'd wished to
be on a battlefield, taking a toll on the Federals.

They didn't know much about the man they were

pursuing. His name was Tom Cooper, he was a Yankee, and he had shot the youngest member of their family. In Cal's opinion, the latter was more than enough reason for him to die.

Their encampment was some six roundabout miles south and very little west of where they had forded the Sabine. Ike was unsaddling his bay and thinking of the trail.

"We ain't far behind," he said. "Some of the sign I saw today wasn't very old, maybe a little more than half a day."

James squatted down and poked some sticks into the small flames. "Hope our supplies hold out. We didn't bring much, and his trail's as crooked as an addled snake."

"We'll get him," Bill assured from where he stood leaning against a maple, sharpening his pocket knife. The path Cooper was making wasn't easily followed, but he hadn't really expected it to be after what little he'd seen of the man.

Ike tore off a piece of jerky and chewed it while waiting for the coffee to boil. His voice was low as he said, "When I'm through, he won't be able to shoot another kid."

Cal grunted in pleasant agreement and Dirk grimaced. He looked at James sitting quietly, his frown barely visible by the firelight. Yet he said nothing else, and Dirk, taking his example, remained silent.

The black mustang felt much better than its master in the brisk air, and he jumped and bucked to get the early morning kinks out. Tom clung stiffly to the saddle, quieted its little dance with a tap of the spurs, then headed the animal due west. He liked a horse with spunk. Making a few turns to the north and then back, he used that energy to confuse his trail before returning to the road around midmorning. Now he was fully satisfied at hiding his course.

The sky wasn't pretty, and Tom knew it couldn't be much above freezing. The weather had been rather frigid the last several days, and he hoped for a warm spell soon. Although, it wasn't nearly as cold as what he remembered of Ohio. The dullness of the sky deepened his feeling of loneliness.

The wagon ruts he followed soon drifted north and kept that course until about midday, when they turned back west. A cabin sat off to the right a little past the bend. It was the first home he'd seen since crossing the Sabine, and the place looked to be well cared for.

Without much water left in his canteen, he turned and trotted the gelding toward the building. Tom hoped to be met with friendliness as his gaze played over the area.

The place was easily recognizable as a farm. The house was first, situated a good distance from the road, with a hog pen seventy-five yards to the left. To the rear of the cabin stood a log barn and pole corral. Ten or twelve acres of open field lay beyond and to the right.

As Cooper neared the cabin, two big, yellow curs came from under the porch, barking viciously. The mustang shied and backed away from the noisemakers.

A stout, bronze-faced man of about sixty strode out the door. He wore simple homespun clothing and his voice was coarse. "Jack! Bull!"

The dogs stopped their barking instantly and went up on the porch and sat down. Cooper swung the black around and got it under control.

"Sorry about that," the old man said while petting the dogs. "What can I do fer you?"

"Just passing through and I wondered if you'd let a man fill his canteen."

"We don't have a well." Motioning with his left hand, he added, "But there's a mighty fine spring right yonder. That's where we get our water, and you're welcome to it."

Cooper stepped down and said, "I'd be much obliged." Then he followed the farmer across the open yard and up a little knoll where a tiny smokehouse sat. A small stream of clear water poured merrily from the ground on the other side of the hill. Below was a baygall with water standing around the bases of the trees.

While Tom filled the canteen, he drank from his cupped palm. It was cold and tasty. Then the old man asked the question that he had heard many times.

"You're from up north, ain't you?"

"Yeah," he replied, standing with the full canteen. He dreaded what might come next, but he wasn't ashamed of where he'd come from—his family had been hard workers—and he wanted to be honest. "From Ohio. This is my first look at Texas."

They started back the way they had come. "Been on the trail long?"

"Long enough to get saddle weary."

"The weather of late ain't been none too kind, either. If my predictions are right, it's gonna come a hard freeze tonight. Maybe some snow. You really ought to stay the night. That is, if you ain't got a pressin' appointment somewhere."

Tom was somewhat surprised at the offer. He hadn't noticed the sky for a while, but it did look worse. Shivers ran down his spine at the thought of making a camp in snow. "I don't want to impose," he commented and hung the canteen on the pommel.

"You won't be. There's no room in the house, but there's plenty of clean hay in the barn if you don't mind."

"Not at all. It'd be a heap better than the cold ground."

"Sure it is," the farmer said with a grin. "Just put your cayuse in the empty stall, then come on in. Dinner's almost ready. By the way," he extended his worn hand, "name's Shane Peters."

"Thomas Cooper," he said as he shook the hand. There was strength in the old man's grip that showed he was still very capable of doing labor. "Tom is what most call me. Thanks." Cooper hurried to the barn.

It was larger than it seemed; besides a place to store hay, dry corn, potatoes, and other foods, it had five stalls of which four were occupied. There was a pair of gray mules, a spotted milk cow, and, what particularly caught his interest, a beautiful red sorrel filly. All were definitely well taken care of. Rubbing the mustang down hurriedly with a handful of hay, Tom placed him next to the mare and gave him a portion of shelled corn after watering him at a trough.

With his gear hung up, he started out and noticed a smaller enclosure at the back corner of the building. It was obviously a pen for the cow in order to keep her separate from the other animals when they were getting exercise in the corral.

Shane met him at the door of the cabin. "Come on in, dinner's ready." Pointing to a dark-haired woman of approximately the same age as himself, he introduced, "This is my wife, Martha. Our daughter will be out in a minute."

Martha Peters greeted him with a friendly smile. She was a strong woman, worn by hard work throughout her years, but still feminine. Tinges of gray along her temples and the lines in her face were the only signs of her age.

Cooper took off his hat and said, "Howdy, Ma'am. I sure appreciate you both letting me stay."

"Nonsense," she scolded with another smile. "We don't have many visitors, and besides, a man doesn't have any business sleepin' out in this weather. Do sit down."

Tom hung his duster and hat on the rack Shane pointed to and took a seat, surveying the room. It didn't differ from any other average farmhouse he had seen. There were two small windows on the front wall, one on either side of the door. A lone one was set into the back wall. At the right end of the long room there was a good-size fireplace, food and dish cabinet, and an oak table which he was seated at in one of four straight-backed chairs with deerskin bottoms. At the left end, a spinning wheel, small bed, and two rocking chairs completed the furnishings. A doorway to another room lay beyond.

They aren't wealthy, Tom mused, *but they do seem comfortable. And that's more important.*

His thoughts were interrupted when a young woman in her early or mid-twenties swished into the room. He stood as Peters introduced them.

"This is our daughter, Belle. Belle, this here's Tom Cooper."

"Nice to meet you," she asserted and smiled a smile that was every bit as gracious as her mother's. Her rich olive complexion accentuated her beautiful brown eyes and hair, the latter of which fell past her shoulders. She was delicate, but definitely not frail like so many other women.

"Well, let's eat before it gets cold," Martha suggested, motioning to the steaming food on the table.

Cooper's and the attractive girl's eyes broke contact as they sat and concentrated on the meal: baked sweet potatoes, fresh corn bread and butter, turnip greens, and fried salt pork. Shane Peters said grace before the food was dished out. Remembering his table manners, Tom found the company enjoyable.

Conversation dealt with farming, Tom's line of work, and then the war. These people held no animosity about the conflict; it had been both sides' fault, Peters concluded, saying it was time to be forgotten.

"It was different with Mexico," he added. "I know,

been here since '35. It got bad, but we made it thanks to Houston and all the other brave men."

Belle was quiet in a shy sort of way, yet she frequently looked at Tom, and once even smiled. Her parents kept the talk lively. Cooper agreed with Shane on the idea of forgetting the difficulties between the North and South.

In fact, the Peterses' friendliness and his own honesty made him finally relate the events in Bentosa. "Even though I haven't seen any sign of them, I'll be headin' out tomorrow. Don't want trouble brought to you," he finished.

"Some men just can't let go of the past," Martha said sadly.

"I wouldn't worry about it too much," Shane consoled Tom. "I've seen the type. Bark's probably worse'n their bite. Likely saw their error when they sobered up."

The farmer's words were reassuring, however, Tom well remembered the barkeeper's opinion of the Landis bunch. And they struck him as being salty upon his first, and hopefully last, encounter.

Belle spoke in her soft voice. "You were lucky that bartender was friendly."

Tom Cooper did not have to ponder the statement. "That I was," he concurred.

"Well, there's always been rough men in this world, and always will be. Goes back to the Bible days." Peters finished his coffee and stood. "I'm goin' to the porch for a smoke. Want to join me?"

Cooper arose and, before retrieving his hat and

duster at the door, said, "That was a mighty fine dinner, Ma'am. Makes a man realize what he's missing after eating his own cooking."

It was even colder and gloomier outside than it had been before he'd gone in. The curs were curled up tightly next to the big live oak in the yard in spite of the openness. Tom and Shane sat in two chairs like the ones at the dinner table, snugging their clothing together and lowering their hats.

With the makings from his shirt pocket Cooper rolled a cigarette and watched Peters pack his homemade pipe. "Does look like this norther is gonna bring some snow."

Shane nodded. "Likely be soon too." Puffing the pipe to life, he added, "Say, you said you worked on a horse ranch. I imagine you saw that little sorrel in the barn, didn't ya?"

"Yessir, she's a beauty. Where'd you get her?"

"Over in Maple Springs. That's the nearest town from here. About fifteen miles north, mainly a farming town. Lot more farms on up the river.

"She ain't been broke. How much would you want fer doin' it? I mean, if you're interested. I'm a little old for that kinda work."

"Sure, I'll do it. But letting me stay the night and all the good grub you serve will be plenty. I'll start right now if you'd like."

Before a gust of wind swirled it away the heavy tobacco smoke hung over Shane Peters's head like storm clouds over a mountain peak. "Let's see what the weather's gonna do, first," he advised.

They sat against the wall on the rough little porch and discussed small matters of interest. While doing so, Cooper marvelled that the dwelling was made from logs, mud, and the strength that this man had put into it in order to have a home while he and his family made their existence from the soil and forest. The smokehouse and barn were constructed in the same way. And all were sound.

Snow began to fall in tiny flakes before either man had finished his smoke. The dogs got up from their unprotected places and went under the porch, walking slowly, as if they wished they didn't have to move. Small gusts of wind from around the corner of the cabin blew some of the particles up on the porch's edge.

With the building as a shield to block the north wind off them, the men continued to talk despite the chill air. Besides, the conversation was good, and company seemed to have been just the thing to diminish Tom's lonely, solemn mood. Finally the topic came back to the war, and Peters inquired, "Many of your kin die in it?"

Before replying to the still painful subject, Cooper took a last drag on the cigarette and flipped it out into the yard. "The only close relative that died was Sid, my younger brother. A few distant cousins were killed, and my best friend, Matt Bailey. He and Sid both fell at Mobile, Alabama. I was there too." He frowned at the awful memory of the siege.

"Lot of men died in the fightin', good men. I had a nephew in Missouri that didn't make it through," the old man said, then paused, staring out at the weather. The temperature was still warm enough to melt the snow not long after hitting the ground, yet it continued to fall. "Looks like we'll have to wait 'til tomorrow fer you to break that mare. Have more time, anyhow." He stood and went to the steps to knock the ashes from his pipe. "Let's go in. My bones has had enough of this."

Tom quickly complied.

Chapter Four

There was a considerable difference in temperature inside the stout log walls. Warm, cozy heat from the fireplace hit Tom and took the chill out. He once again slipped off the duster, and this time Shane saw the bloodstains on the inside and the small tears in the cloth.

"Man," he exclaimed, "it looks like you crawled into a bear's den with him still in it!"

Tom related the story of his fight with the panther and ended by commenting, "I should've been more careful in a thicket around a river. Especially at that late hour."

The two men had taken seats in the rocking chairs while the women were busy in the kitchen. However,

40

Belle heard the story and stated, "It's a wonder you weren't killed."

"That's a fact," her father agreed. "I've been here a long time and only killed two. Seen more, but they sure are hard to get a clean shot at. Last one I got was trailin' me while I was hog huntin'. Lucky for me Jack and Bull smelled him before he got too close. They lit out after him, and the fight was on.

"I tell you, Bull's still got the battle scars from that day. When I stretched that cat out he was ever' bit of seven feet from his nose to the tip of his tail."

The farmer's eyes glowed as he relived the past. "You'll need something fer them cuts." He turned to the women. "Belle, bring over that bottle of red liniment."

The slender young woman with the eyes of a fawn brought the medicine over to Tom from its perch on the mantle. Their hands touched when Tom took the bottle, and she looked away with an embarrassed smile. Tom felt a warmness toward her that made him uneasy. It wasn't like with other women he'd met. He forced himself to look away as she returned to the kitchen.

"Use that before you go to bed and make sure those cuts heal," Peters directed. "Maybe you ought not try to handle that mare tomorrow."

"Thanks. They haven't been nearly as sore as I figured they would, and I reckon I can do it."

Martha and Belle joined them in conversation while the evening meal was cooking. Cooper was more relaxed than he had been in days. Belle asked if he was going to stay the following night after working with the sorrel, and he thought he detected a faint hint of hope in her voice. He shook it off as imagination and said it depended on how tough the mare was to break.

Time passed quickly, and Shane glanced out the window and stood. "Gettin' late. And it looks like the snow's decided to stick. I better go tend to the animals."

Tom went with him and found that the temperature had indeed dropped enough to keep the snow from melting. A layer of white covered everything that wasn't sheltered. The two sauntered to the barn, their boots crunching along. Late sunshine gave the powder on the roof a silver glow.

Tom helped in preparing all the animals for the night. "Got a pretty good operation here," he surmised while Shane milked the cow.

"Enough fer us to keep busy. Especially in the growing season," Peters concluded, deftly squirting the warm milk into a pail. "Butchered the calf a couple weeks ago. Stan Waters helped us dress it out, so I halved the meat with him. He's a Hasinai Caddo that mainly makes his living by huntin'. Other than raising a little patch of corn and taters, that is. He's our closest neighbor and lives by hisself. Fact is, there ain't too many people in these parts."

Peters showed Tom where the clean hay was before closing the heavy log doors and leading the way back to the cabin. It was quite dark by that time, and the yellow light from an oil lamp added to the illumination of the fireplace. The smell of good food was everywhere again as Belle helped her mother set the table for supper. It was suddenly apparent to Cooper that this pretty girl would make some lucky fellow a good wife.

During the meal he and Shane talked of getting an early start the next day with the red sorrel. Belle had made a superb apple pie that Tom savored a large piece of with his last cup of coffee. With a full belly and a warm spirit, Cooper thanked them again before starting for the wonderful bed of hay.

"You be sure and come first thing in the mornin' and eat breakfast," Martha offered. "There'll be plenty."

As Tom had thought, the combined comfort of the hay and doctored cuts drifted him swiftly off to sleep. And surprisingly, his last thoughts were not of the Landises. They were of none other than Belle Peters.

Ike had ordered camp made only a scant five miles from the Peterses' farm. A few hours before dark they had come to where Cooper made camp the night before. Up to that point his tracks were easily read on the soft dirt of the wagon road. However, the trail led off into the timber from their quarry's camp instead of returning to the worn path like all had assumed it would. Now it seemed that the Yankee had begun his aimless wandering again, and the snow-blanketed ground further cast down their hopes of finding his trail again.

James cursed harshly. "See what you've done, Ike?

We're freezing in some God-forsaken thicket! Why don't you give it up? We'll never pick his sign up after this snow melts."

"Stop your whining," Ike ordered in an unusually quiet tone, letting out cigarette smoke with the words. "I'm here, too, ain't I?"

"I'm not whining. But you didn't have to drag us all with you into this death trap."

"So *you* don't want to go after Randy's killer?" Cal asked.

"Appears that way," Ike deduced smugly. "Well, you and Dirk both go on back and get nice and comfortable at home. We'll finish it."

"Randy wasn't murdered, but that isn't the point." James paused, trying to choose words that wouldn't make him and Dirk look like cowards, which they weren't. "I just don't believe it's goin' to be as easy as you think to get that fella. You get too sure of yourself and you're liable to get dusted before he does."

Ike Landis took a long pull from the whiskey bottle that sat beside him. "I ain't scared. Maybe y'all are. He don't have a chance in hell against all of us at once."

Although his face was dark with anger and frustration, James seated himself and drank a cup of laced coffee.

Bill wanted to say something, but he had learned a long time ago not to interfere in other men's quarrels. Particularly brothers. He was very close to all of them or he wouldn't be making this trip, nevertheless, he kept out of their disputes.

The night was shrouded with the heavy silence of unvented fury, and Dirk felt like a peacemaker. "All we can do is keep tryin' to cut his sign. Most farms are up by Maple Springs, maybe he went that way. Just didn't take the road. If we don't find anything by tomorrow night, we can drift up there."

Everyone looked at him with a little surprise, but Ike was first to concur, then the rest. The eldest felt somewhat elated at Dirk's change in ideas. Now, if he could just get James entirely on his side. . . .

The only thing they all saw unanimously in the same light, however, was that it was a cold, miserable night.

Tom Cooper ate breakfast by lamplight at the Peterses' table. Belle looked just as radiant at this early hour as she had the previous afternoon. The lack of loneliness the night before had made it the best in a long time for him.

At the first good light of day, Shane and Tom were in the corral readying the mare. The former tied her securely to a post at one side of the pen. Shane had obviously accustomed her to the bit, for she did not seem to mind. However, her brown eyes grew wide as Cooper placed an old sack over her face to help calm her. She trembled when the saddle blanket was draped over her back and sidestepped as Tom put the saddle on and snugged it down, but the short tether Peters fastened did its job, not allowing much movement except for her rear end.

Tom had been mumbling soothing words and petting her continuously, always keeping contact with the animal if he was near—many a man had received a vicious kick by surprising a nervous horse with a sudden touch or word—but he fell silent upon swinging aboard. His weight made the mare strain to break free and begin fidgeting violently. Squeezing tightly with his legs, Tom gripped the bridle reins with both hands and nodded to Shane for her release.

Safely outside the corral fence, Peters snatched the covering from her face and jerked the rope free of the post in one swift motion. After a starting jump, the mare charged in circles with Tom clinging to her back. The enclosure was roughly twenty by forty yards in size, and the red sorrel bucked around the entire perimeter, Cooper pulling back hard on the reins to keep her head up so that she couldn't get all of her power into the pitches.

Suddenly the animal went into a tight bucking spin, then sunfished over to the fence, trying to scrape her tormentor off. When there was only a foot of clearance between Tom's right leg and the pine poles, he jerked violently back toward the center of the pen and succeeded in turning the mare just in time to save a possible injury.

Yet Tom wasn't prepared as she went into another spin, and the stocky little beast managed to get her head down, hunching her shoulders when her hindquarters exploded upwards. Man and animal separated, the former flying over the latter's head to land on his right hip in the dirty snow that still covered the ground. He instantly rolled to his feet and ran for the fence. Although a savage fighter, the young horse didn't come for him with hooves bent on revenge like others had; she was content enough at being rid of her rider.

"You all right?" Shane asked over the fence.

Tom Cooper laughed. "Yeah, but I'm glad I took my gun off. Could've broken a hip." He looked at the mare in the far corner. She stood nervously, not relishing the feel of the leather seat on her back. Even though the air was quite chilly, sweat had formed on her glossy coat as it had on Tom's brow.

"She's feisty all right." He went toward her slowly and carefully. He would tame her for this friendly old man.

And so he did. It was the latter part of the morning when he was able to steer her over to where Shane sat on the fence. The snow was now almost gone from the ground, adding to its muddiness. Sweat now covered both Cooper and the horse.

He leaned forward and patted her neck. "She wasn't nearly as bad as some I've seen. Make a good mount. A man would pay a high price for her. Nothing but pure strength on these four legs."

"Best ridin' I've seen in a long time," Shane declared.

"Sure you won't let me pay something fer your trouble?"

Cooper thought of all the friendliness and hospitality shown to him from this man and his family. "You've already paid me enough." He stepped down. "She'll be a little frisky whenever you get on her, but not as bad. Once you show 'em who's boss, they usually remember.

"Let's take her in and rub her down. Don't want her gettin' sick," Cooper said and started toward the barn door.

Peters followed. "I sure appreciate it."

The two men stood inside the huge entrance removing the gear and rubbing the sorrel with hay to dispense the sweat. From the opening Tom saw a tall man with dark skin and coal-black hair, which reminded him of his mustang's shiny coat, approach from the tree line on a hardy dun. The man was clad in buckskins with no hat, but a robe of bear hide was around his shoulders. His dark eyes were piercing, and a bow laying across his legs finished the impressive figure.

Peters smiled and waved. "How you doin', Stan? Ain't seen you in a few days."

The Indian slid gracefully to the ground. "Good. Been hunting. How are you and the women?"

"Just fine," Shane replied. Turning to Cooper, he introduced him to Stan Waters. They shook hands. "Had any luck?" Peters questioned the Caddo.

"Real good. Got a buck day before yesterday and two big gobblers yesterday morning."

Cooper could tell right off that the man was friendly. The trio talked of hunting and the mare, while Shane and Tom finished with her and let the other animals into the pens for some exercise. Waters's voice was smooth, and Tom noticed that his English was excellent, considering. It was kind of choppy, but he could just be a man that didn't like to waste words.

"Tom," Peters said when the chores were complete, "why don't you stay another night so we can all go huntin'? That is, if y'all want to and you don't mind sleepin' in the barn again."

There was a pause. Cooper had presumed he would be on the trail again in an hour or so. To exactly where, though, he was far from being certain. And in the back of his mind he really wanted to stay. He wondered if Belle was part of the reason. Besides, the Landises were probably still back in Louisiana and his fears on the subject had been for naught.

"It does sound good, if you're sure I wouldn't be imposing."

"Bah," Peters chided. "After what you did for me? And anyway, you couldn't get very far down the road by dark. Half the day's gone." Stan nodded at his questioning look, and Shane concluded, "Good. Let's eat a bite and we'll hunt till dark. Stan, you can just bunk in the barn tonight, too, if you want."

Tom believed Belle was happy at learning he was staying. These people were really nice, he deduced over a hearty dinner. Belle was more talkative than the day before, and Tom was glad he'd excepted the invitation since otherwise there was nothing else for him to do but continue his lonely drifting. That could wait.

Cooper broke himself away from Belle's melodious voice to check his Spencer. Surprisingly, she joined him in the living area of the cabin. They talked a little about East Texas—the part she was familiar with—

and she finally asked, "Did you do much huntin' in Ohio?"

"Oh yeah. There was plenty of game around the area I lived. But it's been over four years since I was back home. You see, my parents died while I was off in the war."

"I'm sorry." The look on her face made him feel better about being so open. It was easy to be comfortable with her.

"Way of life." He shrugged. "I do wonder what the old place looks like, though. One of my uncles paid me for the farm and took over running it."

Shane Peters rose from where he'd been talking with the Caddo and took down an old flintlock rifle, powder horn, and pouch of homemade bullets from over the door. "You ready?" he asked Tom.

"Whenever you two are." He came over to look at the rifle. "I haven't seen one of these since my pa's."

The farmer patted the stock of the muzzleloader. "Best gun there is, Son. A mite slow to load, but good for way over a hundred yards. And that ball packs a wallop, too."

"Hope y'all get a deer," Martha Peters said. "It's been some time since we've had fresh venison."

Shane explained to his wife, "We're gonna make a good round, so it'll probably be dark before we get back."

"Good luck," Belle said, her eyes fixed on Tom as they exited the house.

So they wouldn't have any problems with the newly broken horse, Peters decided to ride one of the gray mules. When the three men were mounted they started due east from the barn. The two dogs began to follow, but their master gave them a stiff command and they turned back.

It was a surprisingly short distance straight through the woods to the Sabine River, and the group made good time, riding abreast with several yards between each horse in hopes of flushing a deer from its midday bed. Tom felt good in the warm sunshine as he guided the black around dense thickets and through the huge stands of timber.

Though seeing many rabbits and squirrels, they reached a bluff on the river without coming upon a deer or a turkey. From there Shane led the way upstream for half a mile before pulling up in a well-worn game trail. Recent tracks of deer and wolves were plainly evident in the soft soil.

"Tom," Peters whispered, "why don't you find a place to stand, and we'll circle around to try to drive somethin' out over you?"

Cooper readily agreed, and in seconds he was alone, squatted a little way from the mustang with a lengthy view of the trail. The way was dotted liberally with French mulberry bushes, oak saplings, yaupons, and other types of chaparral. Tall trees of every sort protruded grandly above the lower vegetation, making an animal haven.

As he waited, eyes scanning the surroundings and dim lane, his thoughts went to Belle. She was indeed very attractive, and seemed to like him somewhat. He shook his head to clear the subject from his mind. He didn't even have a job. How could he think of getting involved with a woman? It was foolishness.

Tom heard something walking several times, and once got excited at a glimpse of movement which turned out to be a cottontail. More than an hour passed while he sat comfortably against a large pine. The events of the previous days seemed unreal now in his peaceful mood.

Soon Peters returned. "Stan hung back some," he said. "See anything?"

"Not what we're after. You?"

"Small buck got away before I could get a shot off." He glanced down the trail. "Here comes Stan. Let's see what he thinks we ought to do."

The Indian had had the same luck as Tom and suggested that they ride to where a creek emptied into the Sabine a short distance north.

"Yeah, that's the same one that runs behind my field," Shane explained to Tom. Tom. "We can follow it back and go home that way. Maybe we'll jump something and get back before dark. There's a good bit of daylight left."

With weapons held ready, the horses were kept to a slow walk. Cane mixed with the brush that grew in the low area at the mouth of the creek. The waterway was only five or six feet wide at the most. In spite of the wet weather, it didn't look very deep to Tom.

Halting, he said in a whisper, "I'll cross over and ride along the other bank so we'll have both sides covered."

Waters and Shane agreed and Tom quickly forded

the stream. Cypress trees stood here and there, their knees protruding the water's surface in places and causing ripples. Underbrush and cane occasionally blocked his view of the other two.

The creek meandered beautifully by, and Tom rode lost in thought. Two miles further, he entered a small opening. His companions could be seen clearly on the opposite side. Cooper was busy looking for animal sign when something moved in the pine saplings no more than fifteen feet ahead.

The black's ears were pricked when its master brought the Spencer to his shoulder, and suddenly Tom was taken by surprise as the gelding shied from a dark form that burst forth from the thicket. Horse rearing beneath him, he slipped backwards off the saddle, his finger pulling the trigger at the same moment. The bullet went harmlessly into the treetops, and Cooper hit the ground with a thud, flat on his back.

Chapter Five

T om rolled away from the hooves of his fleeing mustang and saw a huge, black boar charging toward him, grunting and rattling his teeth viciously. With a splash the Caddo was across the creek and sliding the dun to a halt between Tom and the hog. The beast wheeled at the appearance of the other intruder and ran back for the cover of the brush. As Stan jumped to the ground, the loud report of Peters's muzzleloader split the air.

"You all right?" Waters queried in concern.

Cooper was gaining his feet. "Yeah. Just a little jarred."

"Dang!" Shane exclaimed as he joined them, already packing another charge into his rifle with the ramrod. "I missed him!"

54

Tom laughed. "Fallin' off a horse many times like that is liable to kill a man."

Waters rode off to retrieve the black while the others searched for blood to be sure Peters hadn't hit the boar. There was none, and Shane thought aloud, "Jack and Bull could sniff out that hog real quick. I got about thirty head of hogs in these woods and I saw that one good enough to know his ears wasn't marked. Dangerous having him around, looked as wild as they come. Could've cut you to shreds."

"Wouldn't be good for eating, but it'd sure make an exciting hunt," Tom said.

Cooler air had settled in, foreshadowing the coming of night, when Stan rode up with the mustang. Before continuing up the creek, Peters asked if they wanted to go after the boar the next morning with the curs. Cooper was enjoying himself and readily agreed.

"Fine," Stan said. "Nothing else to do this time of year."

Shane's mule was also carrying the burden of a yearling doe when the three reined in at the cabin. He'd killed it at dusk, in a grove of pin oaks, less than a mile from the farm. By lamplight, they tied the gutted carcass high in the live oak out front—the temperature was cold enough to keep the meat until it could be dressed the following day—and then took their mounts to the barn.

Martha and Belle were pleased over the kill and listened with interest about the incident with the boar as they served another bountiful meal. Tom thought he could detect another look of gladness in Belle's eyes when she learned that he wouldn't be leaving early the next morning.

After the meal, Peters lit his pipe and announced, "Fellas, since I killed that deer, I think I'll stay here tomorrow and start jerking some of the meat. But y'all go on and take the dogs after that hog."

"I'd hate to go without you," Cooper remarked. "What with them being your dogs and all."

"Nonsense. Stan's worked 'em with me before. Long time ago his people hunted buffalo and routed out bear with dogs." Waters nodded over his cup of coffee at his friend's words, and Shane added, "Enjoy yourselves."

Cooper consented and could hardly believe his good fortune at stopping at this farm. He felt more at home here than he had anywhere since coming south. And he found himself dreading the time when he would ride on.

Finally, after an hour more of relaxing talk, he and Waters retired to the barn.

Ike Landis was leading the way through a soggy flat, his disgust seething at not having recovered Cooper's sign all day, when a gunshot echoed through the timber. He pulled up and pointed ahead to the right, his face dark, as another sounded.

"Bet that bastard's huntin'," he muttered, turning the bay's head. "No more than a mile or two off."

"Hell, Ike, that's probably some farmers out deer huntin'," James speculated. "Couldn't you tell that was two different rifles?"

"Maybe." He really hadn't noticed. He was excited that they now had something to work with. "But just how many farms have we come across so far?" There was no reply, and Ike spurred into motion. "Uh-huh. Let's *find out* who it is."

Lips in a hard line, James brought up the rear.

At the place where Cooper had the mishap with the boar, Ike and Bill dismounted to study the three sets of horse tracks.

"One of these has got to be his," Cal stated.

Bill said, "One of 'em ain't shod."

Dirk didn't like what he saw. "He's met up with some friends. He may even know we're trailin' him by now. He sure is stayin' close."

Ike swung up, started following the tracks up the creek, and directed, "Go easy. I want to see them before they see us."

It was deathly still, the last light of day quickly waning. They rode steadily along. Each man's nerves were on edge at not knowing how close they were from the trio of riders, and the sudden, nearby crack of a rifle at dusk spooked them as much as their horses.

"Where the hell did that come from?" Bill demanded after getting his mount under control.

Cal Landis's dark eyes were wide. "Too close to tell."

"Step down and let your horses rest." Ike's voice was calm. "I heard that bullet connect. We'll give 'em time to get moving again. They'll be headed back to camp, or wherever they're stayin'."

Although his muscles were taught with anticipation as he sat against a willow at the creek's edge, things were clearer for Ike than the rest. His life had always been rough, despite his parents' good examples, and after the war and their deaths, it had seemed to all go downhill. Their farm wasn't near what it had been since the Federals moved in, put a halt to slave labor, and took over the state government. Now this, to him, was just something that had to be seen to, no matter how tough.

Night had almost settled in completely when they resumed their march, the trail of horse sign nearly obscured. The Landises' rifles were drawn, and they hadn't gone far before coming in sight of the Peterses' cabin across a wide field. Its windows were aglow with light which lit up some of the grounds around the building. Ike and his family slipped around the edge of the field, and from some brush near the smokehouse, they watched the trio with their mounts.

"That one over by the dun looks like an Indian," James observed quickly.

"Unshod tracks." Bill grunted as the deer's carcass was hung in the live oak.

Cal was grinning. "That's him. I see that black gelding."

"Here's what we're gonna do," Ike declared when Cooper and his companions disappeared into the house after putting their animals in the barn. "Come daylight, we'll rush 'em. We'll skin out for Bentosa once Cooper's taken care of."

A crude camp was made well into the timber behind

the baygall below the spring. Dirk and James did their part, but were very concerned about the next day. Their minds were eased a little at the thought that maybe the trek would soon be over.

There was no fire made, yet each took a turn at guard duty. Ike felt a calmness during his watch. He was going to enjoy pulling the trigger on this Yankee.

Tom Cooper and Stan had crossed the field and were almost to the creek beyond when the first light tinged the sky gray. The horses found the way through the darkness, the yellow curs trotting behind. Traveling down the waterway on the southern bank, Tom listened to the thrashers come awake as the day dawned.

He and Stan had talked a little before falling asleep the night before, and Tom really enjoyed his company. "Shane said you're a Caddo, is that right?" he asked as they rode.

Waters nodded. "My father was a member of one of the Hasinai tribes. My mother was one of the early settlers on the Neches River. Stan Waters is my whiteman's name. My Caddoan name is Gray Hawk. I chose to take the way of the white man. But I still believe in some of the ways of my father's people."

"I guess some men have probably given you trouble because of what you are, like the Southerners have me." Tom had not told him of the trouble in Bentosa, and started to, then decided to keep it from his own mind.

"Some," the Indian agreed. "But people like Shane and his family are right the opposite."

"They are wonderful," Tom said.

Tom instantly saw the bunch of tracks upon crossing the creek at their goal. He brought them to Waters's attention.

"Probably some other hunters," the Indian dismissed.

In order for the men not to disrupt the hog's scent, they tethered their mounts and sat down to wait for the dogs to hit the trail. The dogs set off at Waters's command, nose to the ground and tails wagging, zigzagging over the little clearing and disappearing into the brush.

It was a beautiful morning, and the scene by the creek was majestic. Sunlight glistened through the pine needles, wet from the melting of the night's frost, and birds sang in the brush.

However, Cooper's mind was no longer easy. It had, for the first time in a while, gone back to the possibility of the Landises following him. Had they? And had it just taken them this long to catch up?

He shook his head and concentrated on talking with Stan. Tom's interest was held by the Caddo more than by many white men he'd talked with, and although it was difficult to put the new horse tracks and Ike's threat from his mind, he still said nothing of it.

The conversation was cut short by the distant barking of the dogs. It came from the direction of the river, and Waters came to his feet and went to his horse. "Let's get to them. I don't want Shane's dogs cut up."

Cooper swung his black in behind the dun, knowing as well as Stan that, if it was the huge boar they were after, the animal wouldn't run far—he would fight. They followed the creek back to the Sabine and, after hitting the muddy bank, stopped to listen. Then the men spurred the horses upstream upon coursing the chase.

Waters halted several hundred yards further and pointed at a wall of brush and cane to their left that was impassable by horses. "They've bayed him. Let's hurry."

With the mustang tied, Cooper advanced with his carbine into the thicket beside Waters with his bow and nocked arrow. The barking dogs were not far ahead, but the going was tremendously slow because the way was so dense. Tom felt clumsy in his heavy boots and spurs compared to the quietness of his companion's soft, deerskin moccasins.

When they were some distance from the river, the surroundings suddenly changed into an open palmetto field. Here and there, strips of cane and tall pines protruded above the sea of fan-shaped grass that grew three and four feet high.

The two dropped to their hands and knees and proceeded toward the fighting sounds, inching through the sharp foliage. They kept below the tops, using only sound to guide them until they were close enough to the action to hear the animals' feet shuffling around. As they raised up to see above the palmetto, Cooper was astounded to see the boar backed up to some thick cane, rattling his teeth and slinging his head, long tusks coming dangerously close to the dogs no more than thirty-five feet from him and the Indian. But the dogs worked as a team and weren't cut.

"Be ready when I holler at 'em," Stan whispered as he began to draw the bowstring.

The .56 Spencer was instantly against Tom's shoulder, hammer back and sights aligned. At Stan's whooping shout the dogs scattered to leave the big boar standing alone. The arrow flew from the bow a split second before the rifle boomed.

Waters petted the dogs, which only had a few insignificant scratches from briars and the palmetto, while Cooper examined the crumpled hog. His shot had done the job of breaking its neck, and the Caddo's arrow was deeply imbedded behind the shoulder.

"Good shots," Tom concluded. "It's a shame the meat would be strong. There'd have been a lot of bacon on that hog."

Waters hung the bow over his shoulder and retrieved the arrow from the carcass. After taking in the boar's size and glancing back the way they had come, he laughed. "We would have had a time gettin' him back to the horses."

Shane Peters was busy skinning the young deer hanging in the live oak when he heard approaching horses. He looked up and saw right off that they were a rough bunch. There were five in all, riding across the yard from the smokehouse with rifles drawn, led by a giant man on a muscular bay.

Peters felt uneasy with only a butcher knife in hand,

nevertheless, he stood firm as the riders charged up and scattered out around him. "Where's Cooper, old man?" the leader demanded roughly, casting a furtive glance at the windows of the log house.

"He ain't here," Shane said truthfully. Tom and Stan had been gone over half an hour.

Ike Landis's temper began to rise. "What do you mean, he ain't here? He's wanted for murder in Bentosa, and I seen him here last night!" He pointed his Henry repeater at the farmer. "I don't know what your relationship with him is, but I'm only gonna ask you once more. *Where* is Tom Cooper?"

Without a doubt Peters knew their identity. There were no badges on them anywhere in sight, and his mind whirled, yet his face didn't change. "Said he was passin' through, and I let him bunk here awhile. He left this morning, way before daylight. Said he was headin' west, maybe for the New Mexico Territory."

"Bill, James, check the cabin. Dirk, you and Cal check the barn." Ike glared at the old man as the others hurried to follow his others. "If you're lyin', you'll wish you hadn't. Shouldn't let a Yankee stay at your place, anyway. Like being a traitor."

Shane's insides tightened at wondering if any of Tom's belongings would be visible to the two at the barn. Bill and James came out of the cabin with the women ahead of them. "Ain't nobody inside except these two," Bill said.

Martha asked, "Shane, what's happening?"

"It's all right. I'll tell you later," her husband replied, his gaze still on Ike.

There was a lengthy silence before Cal and Dirk rode around the house shaking their heads. "He's not in the barn," Cal confirmed.

Ike spat and cursed. "All right, we'll try to cut his sign west of here. Shouldn't take us long." He looked at the woman, then back to Shane, his face cold and hard. "You'd best hope we find his trail."

Nothing more was said, and the men poured out of the yard as fast as they had appeared. Peters stared after them, his wife and daughter doing likewise from the porch.

The sun lacked little more than an hour to reach its zenith when Cooper and Stan drew rein at the cabin. Peters strode quickly out to meet them, and Tom knew something was wrong—the older man's face was laden with worry.

"What's happened?" Cooper asked. His voice was terse.

"They came after you," Shane said, and then explained.

"God," Tom said, looking up at the bright sky. "I should've never stayed here."

"Don't worry over it, just get moving. Ain't no tellin' how soon they'll know I lied." Shane handed him a cloth sack. "Here's some smoked bacon and fried deer steak. It ought to hold you awhile."

Cooper turned to the Caddo. "Stay with them for a time. There may be trouble. Shane can explain." The Caddo nodded solemnly, and Tom shook Peters's hand, directing, "If they come back, tell them *exactly* which way I went, north. Thanks for everything."

Cooper dismounted at the barn long enough to gather his saddlebags and bedroll, which he'd fortunately opted to place in an empty flour barrel on his first night there. How glad he was now. His mind felt numb as he tied the gear in place.

Before spurring the black across the field, he looked back over his shoulder. Belle stood at the corner of the cabin, her dark hair gently moving in the light north wind. Tom raised a hand in farewell and started off at a lope with a head full of many different emotions.

The mustang had carried him five or six miles before he pulled up and thought, *What am I running for?* He hadn't murdered that boy! Five men were hunting him vengefully for nothing more than defending himself.

The last two days had been great. The Peterses had made him feel at home, and he was comfortable. Now he was being made to leave all that, never to return. The Landises would come back to get the truth, angry that they had been deceived. And they weren't above doing harm to the family. Why didn't he stay and fight?

Tom nudged the gelding northeast, now only at a walk. The answer was simple: If he made a stand there, the entire farm and all of the innocent people could very likely be destroyed and killed; it wasn't a place to be easily defended. Maybe the Peterses would be all right if Shane wouldn't hesitate in sending them his way.

Cooper halted a scant distance from the river in a little opening surrounded by brush and cane. Nothing could approach without him or the gelding detecting the movement through the dense cover. He prepared the animal for a stay and sat down against his saddle to eat the fried venison and drink the spring water that was still in his canteen.

Other than some saved money and the cherished friendship of the four people he'd recently met, Tom had nothing. He did not want to ruin the rest of his life by running. It would be better to die.

The Landises were good trackers, obviously, and it shouldn't take them long to be on him, once set in the right direction. If they wanted him, darn it, let them find him here.

He tried to relax. The Spencer lay across his legs.

By the end of the day Ike and the others had searched for Cooper's trail over a vast area to the west of the farm. It was done in vain. There was absolutely no evidence that any traveler had gone that way since the snow, even on the wagon road, and Ike was boiling mad as he sat quietly chewing jerky by the campfire.

Cal said the obvious after picketing the horses. "That sodbuster lied."

Bill nodded his head, and James and Dirk, after looking at each other, also had to agree. The latter was more than a little tired of the trek. Something told him that they were making a big mistake by chasing this

Northerner, but he was sick of futilely voicing his opinion.

"That old man will tell the truth after we're finished in the mornin'," Ike stated.

"As wet as the ground still is, we'd have cut his sign by now," Bill said. "*If* he would've told the truth to begin with. Now we're another whole day behind!"

"I don't want an innocent family hurt," James said levelly. "They're poor, and Cooper probably offered 'em money for letting him stay."

Ike Landis sneered and smiled in that evil way Dirk didn't like. "Innocent? Guess that's why they were all off a-huntin' like old friends. Hell, that Indian's likely wherever Cooper is now. You don't worry yourself over that farmer."

Chapter Six

The early-morning air was cool but not freezing. Cooper was thankful for the warming trend. He was nervous and restless, though. He'd remained in the small clearing ever since stopping, save for going to the river once for water, and the sitting was getting to him.

After finishing some of the bacon and a pot of coffee, he loaded his gear on the gelding and left the smoldering fire to make a small circle around the camp. Although he was still resolute in his decision to wait for the inevitable confrontation, he wanted something to do, to help pass the time and keep his mind clear.

He saw plenty of wildlife during the short ride, but no sign of his position being approached by humans.

His route from the farm wouldn't be hard to follow. Were the Landises already onto it? Were Belle and her parents all right?

Slipping the bit from his mustang's mouth so it could crop some of the brown grass back in the encampment, he left the saddle on and planned to make the same round later in the day. If it had to be—and it seemed it did—Tom yearned for the fight with the Landis family to be done with soon.

Dirk brought up the rear as they circled around the farm to the barn. Ike had aroused them long before dawn and he'd said little during the dark ride, and nothing to clarify what he had in mind. The air was crisp and the light quickly increasing as Ike guided his bay to the front of the building, yet lamplight still emanated from the cabin across the backyard. So far they were undetected, but Dirk's jaw hardened when Ike stuffed a piece of cloth down the neck of a half-empty whiskey bottle.

"Let the animals outta there," the big man ordered in a low tone. "No sense in killin' good stock."

James and Dirk made no move, only sitting their mounts nervously, so Cal and Bill followed the command. "You gonna burn it? That's their living," Dirk said.

Ike Landis was angered by his brother's opposition once again. "Our baby brother's laying in his grave, and now his murderer might've got away because of that farmer! That old man is gonna talk straight this time."

The many mixed feelings of Dirk and James kept them skeptical but nevertheless silent. Two gray mules, a pretty red sorrel, and a spotted cow came charging out ahead of Bill and Cal, heading for the timber. With the flick of his thumbnail, Ike struck a match and lit the cloth that hung from the whiskey bottle. It left his hand with a heave and shattered into flames against the inside wall of the barn and ignited the hay scattered beneath. Ike wheeled the bay harshly and spurred hard for the log house.

Breakfast was just being completed, the Peterses and Stan in somber moods over Tom's hasty departure, when the dogs began barking. As Shane and the Caddo stepped out on the porch, Martha shouted from inside, "The barn's afire!"

A rifle cracked and a dog yelped in pain. The barking instantly subsided. Shane retreated long enough to grab the rifle, powder horn, and bullet pouch over the door and to tell his wife and daughter to stay put, then rushed back out. Waters was right behind with his bow and quiver of arrows.

The hammer was back on the flintlock as Peters gained the yard. Riders poured around the building, and Shane, seeing Ike in the lead, fired. The shot was in haste and went wide of its mark. Ike's Henry bellowed and was on target. Grunting, the old man crumpled to the ground.

James steadied his gelding, carbine pointed in the Indian's direction across his legs, and murmured, "Lord, God."

Waters was drawing back an arrow when Bill pointed his rifle directly in his face. "Don't do it! Drop it!"

Stan let the weapon fall to the earth, then turned to where Shane was lying. "How bad?"

Peters replied through clenched teeth, "Don't know. It's my leg."

The women appeared at the door. They rushed out with a cry at the sight, Martha kneeling by her husband's side.

"Better be glad it *is* your leg, old man," Ike snarled.

Martha looked up at the rider on the huge bay and asked, "What do you want?" But she really knew.

"That's very simple, Ma'am," he drawled. "We just want to know which way that Cooper fella went. And we don't want any more lies like we got last time!"

The crackling of the burning barn was tremendously loud in the stillness. Shane Peters looked at him from pain and anger-stricken eyes. Despite the situation, he didn't want to send the group after Cooper so soon after he'd left.

"Darn you!" he blurted. "I'll not tell you. Why don't you leave him alone?"

"I don't think you understand." Ike motioned to Cal and said, "Torch the cabin."

The younger man dismounted and lit another fire-bomb that was already prepared. Belle shrieked in protest and ran between him and the house. As he shoved her roughly aside, Waters lunged forward, and Shane yelled, "No! You dirty—"

His hate-choked words were cut short as Martha

screamed when the stock of Ike's rifle connected soundly with the side of the Indian's head. Stan fell in a heap almost under the bay's prancing hooves, and the front wall of the cabin burst into wicked yellow and orange flames at the same moment.

Cal swung aboard his mount, grinning as maliciously as his oldest brother, while the Peterses stared in horror at the burning building. The heavy smoke curled upwards to mix with that of the flaming barn, and a north wind hurled it all southward.

Ike rode up close to Shane and leered down at him. "Now we'll try it again. Which way did he go?"

"North, north! And I hope he kills all of you!"

"Not likely, old man," Cal piped up.

"I think he's finally being truthful," Ike said almost pleasantly. He reined his mount wide of the burning house and led the way toward the field.

Both Martha and her daughter had tears streaming down their cheeks, but the former sobbed and stepped nearer her home. "No, Martha! It's gone, honey, it's gone. Y'all get Stan further away from it before it collapses."

The women managed to move the strong body of the Caddo over close to Shane. Blood matted his dark hair over his left ear, but his breathing was slow and steady. Belle tried to wake him to no avail while her mother checked Shane's leg. No bone was broken by the .44 slug, just an ugly, bleeding hole punched diagonally through the muscle.

The old walls of their home suddenly gave way, sending sparks and ashes swirling up, and made the women's sobs harder to choke back as they headed toward the smokehouse shed for some old scraps of cloth and a pail for water from the spring. The men's wounds were their first priority.

The cold rag that Belle touched to Stan's head brought a groan, and even before Martha was through with Shane's wound, the Caddo was sitting up groggily while Belle bandaged his head. He took a long look at the ruins of the family's home. "I'm sorry, Shane."

"It ain't your fault. You all right?"

"Little dizzy. But it could be worse."

Stan struggled to his feet after his head was taken care of. He stood as wobbly as a newborn colt for a time before thanking Belle for her doctoring. Then he stared over the shambles of the cabin to those of the barn. Only parts of the corral and cow pen were standing.

Peters thought aloud, "Since we didn't hear nothin' of the animals screamin' to get out, I reckon they turned 'em loose first. Only decent thing I can see in that bunch.

"Stan, I wouldn't ask if I could ride. But do you think you could find your horse and catch up to Tom before those roughs do? I just don't believe he killed their brother without reason. I want him to know they're onto him."

Waters nodded, deep understanding on his face. "I'll make it. You can stay at my place."

"Thanks for the offer, and we'll probably have to take you up on it later, but I want to be sure that's the last we see of them snakes. Don't want to jeopardize your place. I think there's enough old stuff under the shed for us to rough it along the creek for awhile."

Peters took a deep breath and shifted his hurt leg as he finished, "If you don't find Tom pretty quick, come on back. I just want to make sure he's got a good lead on 'em. Tell him to get plumb out of the country if you find him. They won't stop till they get blood."

Waters steadied himself, trying to ignore the pounding in his skull. "I'll try to find my dun," he said, picked up his bow, and walked toward the ruined barn.

Shane called after him, "You be careful."

Martha and Belle's tears had ceased while they made sure the bleeding stopped on Shane's leg. It finally did, but worry and shock still covered their faces. With their help, Peters gained his feet. He was very weak and he used the rifle as extra support.

"Shane, how will we ever start over?" Martha asked sadly.

Braced on his daughter and wife as they trudged slowly to the smokehouse—the only building left standing—he replied with as much confidence as he could muster, "We'll make it somehow, sweetheart. We always have."

However, he was not at all sure. The farm was almost totally destroyed along with all their stored food, except for the large quantity of meat in the smokehouse. How could he at his age manage to erect another home and barn? It was a hard enough job for a young man. Sure, Stan could be relied on in this time of need, and Martha and Belle were strong women. But it still seemed hopeless.

It was not yet midmorning, but his body felt the need for a long rest. The smell of smoke dampened his mood even more.

Almost a mile to the west, Waters found his horse grazing placidly. He climbed aboard its sleek, bare back, dizziness and nausea flooding over him at the effort. It was a time for speed, and he heeled the mount into a hard gallop, having only pressure from his knees and tugs on the dark mane to guide the animal.

During his forty-two years, he'd had plenty of chances to judge the character of many red, black, and white men, and although he hadn't been around this Northerner long, he agreed with Shane—Tom was honorable. As he clung to his mustang, each jolt shooting a pain through his head, Waters hoped he could make a wide circle and pick up the trail ahead of the Landises.

Tom ate the last of the deer steak around noon, then once again rested against a massive sweet gum and had a cigarette. He could have made it to Maple Springs the evening before. Perhaps there was law there. But it wouldn't accomplish much by hiding behind a sheriff; Ike and the rest would just head out after him again when he left town. No, Cooper would indeed end it here, before any other people got involved.

If only I hadn't gone into that saloon and started

gossiping with the barkeep. It was too late for those thoughts, though.

He rode to the river so the black could drink. His nerves were rigid as he stood beside the horse on the bank, the Spencer carbine in hand. The water level was steadily dropping, but its color was still murky. Drinking it was not pleasurable for humans unless one made strong coffee with it.

Tom Cooper had faced the chance of death many times in his life, especially during the war. He had counted himself lucky to make it through the carnage, but now he wasn't so sure. He'd had a lonely life since leaving Ohio, and now what chance did he have against five men? Though he was better than average with a gun, he never considered himself a gunfighter, and he was none too confident.

Mounting, he walked the gelding slowly southwest. None of his belongings were left at the camp. Almost thirty years of living and all his possessions could be carried with him on a horse. Tom hoped that something would happen soon. At least maybe it would be over then, one way or another.

The Landises weren't far beyond the farmer's field when they hit Cooper's sign. It led due north, and Ike was pleased, feeling no more remorse over what they had just done than if he had only stepped on an ant.

Bill rocked in the saddle for a while, then speculated, "With the time that's passed, it'll likely take us a good bit to catch up again. All these cussed thickets will slow us down." They had already lost the trail once, but quickly recovered it when the undergrowth thinned a little.

Ike's face was set determinedly. *It doesn't matter,* he reflected. *We'll get him eventually.* They had shown that farmer a thing or two. And so they would Cooper.

James rode slumped, vaguely aware of his companions' words, concerned over what had taken place in the early-morning hours. He hated that Randy was dead, but it didn't make what they were doing right. And Dirk was the only one to feel somewhat the same. Yet James would continue on with the trek, because he was bonded by Landis blood and believed in backing a family member's play like always. Whether that member was right or not. Also, he wanted to keep any more of that Landis blood from being shed at the hands of the Yankee.

Dirk, sensing Tom Cooper's ability with a gun, was very worried about the upcoming confrontation. Not that he was afraid of him; Dirk had faced two men with guns over disputes since the war. Both times he'd walked away from their corpses, and it hadn't been murder. But would this be?

After being so close to Randy during their young years, playing, fishing, and hunting, the only thing Cal's mind craved was vengeful justice. He could still hear the report of the Yankee's gun in the confines of the saloon, and then the sickening thud of Randy's body hitting the floor. Cal's young age and the huge odds they had against Cooper made him unafraid, only anxious. Plus, he had the utmost confidence in his oldest brother.

* * *

The Caddo's dun carried him swiftly northeast, and his hawkeyed alertness, which had given him his name, made him pull up the instant his horse intersected the tracks of a lone rider headed due north. They were bound to belong to Tom's black, and Stan relaxed at knowing he was ahead of the Landises as he swung onto the trail. Though they couldn't be far behind, for it wasn't a long way to the farm.

The horse was forced to go at a walk when the sign gradually angled toward the Sabine and into denser thickets. Waters squeezed between almost impenetrable clusters of yaupons, myrtles, and cane. Several yards further there was a clearing that had obviously been used for a camp. Fighting another wave of dizziness, Waters slid to the ground to scout the area.

Remnants of a small fire lay to the left, a considerable number of cigarette butts nearby. There were several faint boot prints in spots, and a horse had been tethered on the other side near a laurel. A confusing array of comings and goings were evident, yet only by one horse, and the Indian expertly picked out the most recent. It surprisingly led a winding course back south after a pause at the river.

"Why would he camp only this far away, and then head back?" Stan murmured. It was puzzling.

Cooper knew one thing for sure, he had made a hell of a jumbled trail in a place no bigger than a square mile. Now, with the gelding well hidden, he was positioned behind a large beech a little way from the river. His back trail was visible for about thirty steps, and he was settled for a wait with the Spencer carbine in the crook of his arm.

All was quiet, but definitely not peaceful. However, he found himself remembering Belle Peter's warm smile. Her beauty was firmly in his mind. He tried to push away the thoughts of her—he would never see her again.

Half an hour dragged by and he became aware of an approaching horse. There were no voices, squeaking of saddle leather, or the rattling of bit chains. But the plodding hooves came steadily on, right down the trail he'd made.

Tom's heart pounded. This was it! Backing the hammer of the carbine, he pressed the stock into the hollow of his shoulder and braced the barrel against the trunk of the beech. The sights were lined on the spot where the first rider would come into view, Tom's finger grew white on the trigger.

Chapter Seven

The first things Tom noticed were the buckskins Stan Waters wore. A slight surge of relief and wonder came over him, then, at the sight of the white bandage around the Indian's head, worry and fear followed. He lowered the gun and stepped into view.

"What's happened?"

Stan showed no surprise at the sudden appearance of Cooper, face only hardened as he halted the dun. His voice was soft and smooth as usual. "You don't have much time. They're on your trail and I'm not far ahead."

His frown deepening, Tom asked, "What happened to your head? Are the Peterses okay?" He dreaded the answer.

Waters related the events in his short, straightforward manner, and Tom's face began to flush with the boiling anger inside him. The story was bad. The Peterses were alive, but the family was far from being all right. It was his fault. Tom shook his head and motioned for Stan to follow as he went to the black and mounted.

The Caddo pulled alongside when he stopped on the wet riverbank. "Shane said to get out of the country. They want blood. And won't quit till they get it. You've got to ride hard." He'd already mentioned where the Peterses said they would stay, and added, "I'm heading back to 'em."

Tom thought for a moment. "Good," he said, eyes fixed on the current. "Someone needs to stay with them since Shane's hurt. Try to hide your trail and be careful.

"Shane's family was great to help me. And now they haven't got a thing because of it. I'm going to face those darned Landises, then I'll be along. If I'm able."

"You sure?"

Cooper nodded, but he wasn't looking at Stan. "I believe in repaying my debts. Thanks."

Although it was dangerous, Stan understood Tom's reasoning. He was torn between the need to hurry back to Shane's distraught situation, and the desire to join this man in his fight. Finally, he said, "Good luck," and swung his dun downstream and into the timber.

Cooper's mind was still in turmoil as he trotted the gelding up the edge of the Sabine. Yet he had a plan.

Mouth set in a grim line, he hoped the Landises were close.

Reaching a place where the bank was swept clean for a full ten yards between timber and water, he plunged the horse knee deep into the river. His tracks were distinct in the soft earth up to that point. That was exactly as he wanted it.

For fifty yards he continued north in the water, then turned into the cane and undergrowth at a bend in the river. With his course now concealed in the brush, he rode quickly back and reined in when the place he had entered the water was visible. A screen of cane and young laurels grew between him and the open bank.

There, after tethering the mustang further back in the thicket, he squatted down with the Spencer. This was a much better position than the previous one, but there he had figured on a fair fight. Now he just wanted to annihilate the devilish clan of Landises for what they had done to Shane and the others.

There was one difference now, though. Before, having been forced to leave his new-found friends, Tom hadn't really cared if the Landises killed him. He had nothing, no one—the loneliness he'd felt before meeting Shane's family had set in with more force— and he thought only of taking out as many of the Landises as possible before he went down. Now, the Peterses needed help rebuilding their homestead, and, if for no other reason, Copper wanted to survive for that.

The trail had been lost again, and the Landis procession was slowed more while unraveling its course.

Dirk was first to see the new set of tracks that converged with Cooper's, and he pointed them out to the rest.

"Whoever it is ain't riding right along with 'im," Bill observed. "Must be that Indian! They ain't shod, and looks like he was traveling mighty fast."

Ike silently agreed to the speed of the rider, the hoofprints were spaced further apart than the tracks they believed to be Cooper's, and bushes were broken in some places. But he wasn't sure about the identity. "I gave that redskin a good knock on the head. And we've got a lead on him. Plus, he would've had to find his horse after he woke up."

"We've been goin' kinda slow. But he *would* have to be damn quick," Dirk consented.

James pulled his Sharps single-shot carbine from the saddle boot, and the other men quickly followed suit. "Better be double careful now, anyhow," he said.

Shortly, the group came upon the campsite in the little clearing. They paused long enough to examine all the clues. Bill found the partial impression of a moccasin which proved beyond any doubt that it was the Indian who was trailing Cooper. There was some disgruntled talk over the matter, and it increased when they discovered that the set of tracks began a gradual wandering back south and west from the river's edge. The trail twisted crazily for about a mile, appearing aimless, as it had right after Cooper first crossed the Sabine into Texas.

Dirk didn't like the looks of what he saw. Their quarry had made camp not even half a day's ride from the farm, then started back in an uncaring manner. And, too, the unknown Indian was ahead of them.

"Sure don't seem very worried about gettin' far away," he surmised, guessing grimly at what Ike would say.

Instead, it was Cal who said with a confident air, "He'll wish he had before we're finished." Then came Ike's affirming grunt.

It wasn't a long wait for Tom, although his anxiety and anger made it feel such. The soft noises of the forest were disrupted by the plodding of horses on the muddy riverbank. Even as the five riders came in sight and Tom cocked the Spencer, he reproached himself for thinking the quiet sounds of Stan's have been those of a large group.

Cooper's gaze settled on the bear of a man astride the magnificent bay. He and the rest were discussing the disappearance of the tracks in whispers. Their faces were burned into Tom's brain, yet it was still hard for him to believe that these men wanted his death enough to do what Waters had described. His fury hadn't calmed and he aimed the carbine at the profile of Ike's unshaven face. This is what he'd wanted upon first hearing about the destruction of the farm.

His thoughts were now more rational, however, and his finger stopped its pull on the trigger. They had started it . . . and he could end it with only. . . . No, he couldn't; it would be murder this way. Maybe there was another way to make them see the light, scare them, something. Whatever, it had to be done quickly. He lowered the barrel of the gun and fired, afraid he would regret it as he did.

The terrific blast shattered the afternoon stillness like glass and the slug kicked up mud under the bay's belly. It reared and lunged, sending Ike sprawling backwards to the ground, still holding firmly to his Henry rifle, Cal's mount, jostled by the other milling animals and frightened further by two more shots high in the air, sunfished violently into the Sabine. Cal went reeling from the saddle into chest-deep water, his long gun was lost in the murky current.

The other three men fought their horses into submission just as Ike was recovering from his impact with the riverbank. His repeater spat two unaimed balls into the brush, and he yelled, "Get him!"

Cooper was mounted and swinging the mustang to the west as Dirk, James, and Bill Landis crashed into the thicket. They rode abreast, several yards between each, rifles back in their saddle scabbards and the easier-operated belt guns in their hands. Bill's curses were cut short as he unleashed flame and lead at the fleeing man and horse twenty yards ahead. James and Dirk's revolvers began barking sporadically. The shots were not aimed, it wasn't possible in the thick foliage and at the speed the men were traveling, they were more or less thrown at their prey.

Upon hearing the pistol reports Tom crouched even lower in the saddle, his mustang going as fast as possible in the brush-choked area. He weaved the animal back and forth to keep the most cover between him and his assailants. Twice, hot lead came close enough to hear. If one of the flying projectiles should connect solidly with the horse or himself, all would be lost, and what he'd just done would have been fruitless. Maybe it was anyway. Those three behind him sure weren't scurrying for safety, it was the other way around.

Limbs, briars, and vines whipped mens' and horses' faces and cut at their flesh. The gunfire lessened and Cooper was certain his gelding had widened the gap considerably. Steam came from its nostrils with each breath, but it hadn't yet begun to lather, and Tom knew the little horse had plenty more strength to call on if needed.

He held his pace and present westward course, occasionally angling south, for several more minutes. The distance increased between the factions so much that he could no longer see movement behind him, and the shots had long since stopped. Yet Tom knew his trail could be plainly read at the rate he was traveling. He would have to throw a kink in it before the black tired.

Suddenly he burst into an area of open woods. A small knoll lay ahead, and Cooper wheeled to the right after dropping below its crest. He soon had to slow to a walk in order to squeeze into another dense wall of chaparral. Dead leaves and pine needles blanketed the ground, and, other than a few broken twigs and bruised plants, his sign of passing was reduced greatly.

The Landises weren't apt to follow his path through the open strip of timber for fear of another ambush, and as they took time to skirt it, he would be laying yet another crooked trail. Also, it was getting late. Secure in this knowledge, Cooper made a slow, wide arc to the west before halting for the night.

After rubbing the mustang down with pine straw, Tom Cooper seated himself on a fallen log to reload the Spencer and think. Had he only wasted time by causing havoc for the men that called him an enemy? Very likely. Or had he shown them that he wasn't to be messed with? He didn't think so.

Tom had totally forgotten about eating and unrolled his blankets. He wouldn't likely get much sleep. He was too concerned over the Peterses. He wanted to return their kindness and help, but he wondered if they were angry with him. No, Shane had sent Stan to make sure he was on the run, out of harm's way.

But what about Belle? Her entire way of life had been destroyed and her father hurt because of him. He felt ill as he lay awake in the chilly night air with his hand on the Colt's walnut grip.

Cal Landis waded out of the river. His clothes were dripping wet and his teeth chattered as he stood next to Ike. He had barely been able to catch his hat before it floated out of his reach. Now he squeezed the water from it and looked at its distorted shape. The wind felt icy and did nothing to help his mood.

He exploded, "I don't believe it! Lost my horse and rifle and now dang dung near freezin' to death! I—"

"Listen!" his brother silenced him. "They're shootin'."

The young man's anger increased at not being able to join in the scrap. "I hope one of 'em plugs him," he hissed.

Situated in the tree line to keep some of the cold wind off of him, he began to wipe his Colt Dragoon down with Ike's bandanna and remove the useless, wet loads of powder and ball. The bullets he put in his pocket. As he did, he listened to the ebbing sounds of the fight and stewed over his breech-loading rifle that was now somewhere on the muddy bottom of the Sabine.

Like Randy, Cal had only started wearing a pistol since the death of their ma and pa. To him, it gave back some of the pride he'd had when their plantation was doing so well before the war. Never had he raised the old weapon against a man, but now he would give anything to get a chance at the Yankee.

He was thinking of having to wait until his mount was recovered to fill the cylinder of the revolver, the powder flask being in his saddlebags, when a disturbing question came to mind. He put it to Ike. "You think that Indian split trails with him to fool us, then circled back to join him?"

The big man was looking deep into the shadows of the forest. "Could have. Could be anywhere. Wish I'd have hit him harder." He unconsciously checked the load in the chamber of his Henry. "Guess that Yankee decided to set a trap for us after that redskin told him what we did."

Ike was furious at having fallen for the old trick, and he couldn't fathom why one of them hadn't gone down. It was as if Cooper was just toying with them. James and Dirk would be even more set against the situation. Unless they managed to get him. God, how he hoped they would.

The light was fading fast when the three returned. Cal, clothing far from being dry, had his back against a red oak, his knees drawn up to his chin, and looked much younger than he was. His face was eager, James thought, like maybe it was finished and they could all go home. He tossed him an almost-empty bottle of whiskey for warmth and actually wished that they could report that news.

Bill was the one to dismount and answer Ike's questions about the events. Dirk was mad, partly with himself at continuing this dangerous foolishness, but mainly at Ike for instigating it. They were lucky beyond reason.

"We could've had our heads blown off!" James voiced the thought that was on all their minds. But only he and Dirk acted concerned over the idea.

"Darn it," Ike muttered as he stared into the distance. "It's almost dark. Some of you find mine and Cal's horses. We'll make camp here tonight and try to find his trail in the mornin'. He'll have a lead, but hopefully not too much."

Dirk and James said not a word as they rode off in search of the escaped mounts. There was no use saying anything; the previous event had done nothing to change their oldest brother's mind. And the deadly chase would be resumed the next day.

* * *

Stan reached the Peterses just as the sun was setting. He had gone by his small, secluded farm to pick up some provisions on the way back, and the dun was spent from the trip. He'd fashioned an Indian-style bridle from some rope. It was a much simpler rig than conventional types, but served the purpose well.

The camp was in a narrow clearing beyond another ridge, not far past the smokehouse and baygall. The creek was still about a mile to the northeast, and Waters figured the old man had decided to stay closer to the spring and his store of smoked meat than the muddy waterway.

Shane sat alone at the opposite edge of the opening on a tattered blanket. His back was to a large pine and his rifle lay across his lap, but there was a tired look on his face as he looked up at the dismounting Caddo.

"Did you get to him?" he inquired.

Stan lowered the bundle on his back to the ground and said, "Yeah. He said he was going to face 'em, then, if he was able, he'd head back. He was pretty torn up over what they done, and said he wanted to pay back the kindness you showed him. And there was a look in his eyes that said he was tired of it."

Peters was worried as he gazed into the deepening shadows.

"God help him. He's a good fella."

Stan said nothing of his urge to stay with Tom. He was definitely needed here. "I brought a few things from my place," he said after hobbling the horse. "Where are the women?"

"Went to hunt enough firewood for the night. It

would've been too hard to tote very much from the shed."

"I'll get some in the morning." The Caddo began unwrapping the pack he'd brought.

The bundle was held together with a leather thong. Two bear hides enclosed three deerskin shirts and a blanket. From the very center of the pack, Stan removed a sack of cornmeal, coffee, and some sweet potatoes. There was also a small quantity of dried herbs which he mixed with a bit of water and started heating in an old kettle the Peterses had retrieved from the smokehouse shed, along with various other articles. He said it would help prevent infection of Shane's wound.

"I can't thank you enough," the farmer stated.

Waters waved away the remark and rose to help the women as they returned with arms full of limbs, pine knots, and other deadfall. Bull, the yellow cur, came padding along behind. After assuring Martha and Belle that his head was fine, Stan questioned, "Where's Jack?"

Shane Peters's face hardened as he answered, "When everything quieted down, Bull led me to him. He was lying gut shot in the woods. I figured as much by the yelp we heard right before the foray. That's what those heathens' first shot was for. It just scared Bull so bad he hightailed it. Can't blame him. I had to finish Jack, he'd have never made it."

A meal was prepared and the camp made much better with the supplies Waters produced. He doctored the raw entry and exit holes in Shane's leg with the paste of boiled leaves, not explaining what they were, yet Peters believed nonetheless in their medicinal qualities. The Indian told again of the meeting with Cooper for the women's benefit, and Belle was not surprised to find herself glad of the fact Tom planned to return.

She remembered the hard look of Ike Landis and worried over Cooper's safety. What chance did he have against five men? It was strange that she did not feel the slightest bit of anger toward this man who had brought so much pain and trouble to her family. Yet her mother and father didn't seem disturbed over his possible return, either. In fact, they seemed to gain hope.

As for herself, Belle prayed for his safe return. There was something about the sandy-haired man in his tan duster that was attractive. Maybe it was his manner or the gentleness that she could detect underneath his rugged exterior.

Chapter Eight

The black was carrying Cooper at a ground-eating canter in a westward circle back toward the farm at the first, gray hint of dawn. More than anything, Tom wanted to help the Peters family rebuild. But how could he do that if the Landises kept after him? Was he now just leading the trouble back to Shane and the rest by not ending it at the river? That would have been plain murder, though, and unlike some men Cooper believed the taking of a human life, even a dire enemy, was not to be taken lightly.

Squirrels barked and popped their tails at him from the safety of the high boughs. Robins and thrashers were busy flipping leaves and pecking on tree roots in search of food. The day before, he had fully expected to be killed—and maybe that would have been best for all involved—but, as the sun's rays started to brighten and warm the earth, he decided that it was a good day to be alive.

Midmorning brought him to what was left of the Peterses' farm. It was sickening. Anger and sorrow gripped his heart. The only complete structures left standing were the smokehouse, adjoining shed, and hog pen. The log barn and house were nothing but black, evil-looking ashes. They still smoldered, and the smell of charred wood and other materials became stronger as he approached.

The faces of the family flashed through his mind. Belle's sweet smile and beautiful complexion lingered the longest and Tom realized, even though he did not know her well, he cared for her more than he wanted to admit. Maybe he would get to know her better, providing he could ever make up for the trouble he'd caused. He vowed to himself that if the Landises should persist with their senseless quest for his death, he would face them directly.

Soon he made out the faint trail the Peterses and Stan had left as they went to their camp. In less than five minutes he topped a ridge and then entered the clearing below. He was met first by Bull. Shane looked weak sitting on the old blanket but smiled at him gladly, and the women stood and came forward.

"Are you all right?" asked the younger of the two.

"I'm fine," Cooper said as he dismounted. His gaze took in each person's expression, seeing hope and worry in all, and finally settled on Peters. "Shane, I can't apologize enough. Stan told me, and I—"

The old man silenced him with an uplifted hand. "He told us, but I don't hold you responsible. Most men would've never looked back."

"Fact is, I shouldn't have stayed at your place," Tom asserted. "And I intend to put things right. I hope I haven't made a mistake by leading my trail back here, but. . . ." After a pause, he related the story of his near killing of Ike.

"God bless you," Martha said. "You proved you're a better man by not murdering him."

"I don't want more bloodshed, but it may come to it. We might not see them again, but if we do, I'll face 'em alone. It's me they want. I want to help rebuild the farm if this trouble passes. I can't leave." Tom took a deep breath and looked at the dun tethered to a laurel. "Where is Stan?"

Belle nodded back the way he had come. Tom turned and saw the Indian exit the timber and brush in the same place he had. Waters's steps were silent.

"I must have ridden right past you!"

"Right under me," Waters corrected Tom. "I was watching from up in a holly. High enough that your horse didn't get wind of me. Stayed awhile to see if you were followed."

It was eerie that he had been so close to another person without knowing it. Yet, under the present circumstances, Tom was more than reassured by Stan's ability. He looked at the sun and said, "I might have been, and they'll have plenty of time to show before dark. I'd like to move the camp to a more secluded spot on the creek—if that's okay with you, Shane—

because I've got a plan. We've got time, I think. I hid my sign pretty good last night. We might even try to make a small shelter."

Cooper made no mention of his idea again, and no one questioned him. They began preparing to move the meager supplies of the encampment. Waters offered the use of his cabin once again, but they settled on making sure the Landis trouble was over, first. Belle noticed that her father was more invigorated since the arrival of Tom, and though danger was still a very real possibility her own spirits were lifted as well.

Cooper was extremely thankful that he'd been greeted so warmly. Stan quickly made Shane a crutch from a forked sweet gum limb, and the little clearing was left behind. There was plenty of evidence that a campsite had been situated there. It was as Cooper wanted it.

With all the discontented feelings of the night before, Ike Landis's bunch was a surly lot. Cooper's trail disappeared from an open stretch of timber into a dense thicket, and it was noon before they came to where he had camped. Horse droppings and tracks were the only signs that their quarry had spent the night. From there, the trail, now a little easier to follow, arced back south, and Ike uttered an oath.

"Dang fool's headin' back toward the farm!"

"No sign of that Indian joining him again, though," Bill put in. "Don't show good sense."

Dirk was tired and disgusted. And it showed in his

voice. "Don't y'all see he's just stayin' far enough ahead of us for our chuck to run out? Darn near has, too! Been livin' off jerky and coffee for two days, and now the coffee's gone.

"He could've nailed some of us back at the river! But no, he's just messin' with us."

His mind already concerned with those facts—he'd had to cinch his own belt up a couple of inches because of the skimpy rations—Ike's anger rose, his proud, confident air taking over. "I'm sick of hearin' your mouth run off like a calf with the scours about what he *could* have done! He didn't, and that's where he made his mistake. If he don't want to die, that is."

All fell silent as they continued along the path Cooper had left. The sun was bright and the day warm enough for the men to shed their coats. They wound through game trails and thickets, crossed small branches and patches of open woods, and the tenseness brought beads of sweat to their brows. Jerked beef, water from the canteens, and a swallow or two of whiskey made up dinner. It was consumed while traveling. Time elapsed gradually, their pace slow and careful, and the ruined farm finally came in sight.

Cal pulled up beside Ike and stared across the field at the sorrel mare, grazing on the brown grass near the eastern edge. "You know, someone would pay a good price for that piece of horse flesh. It's a wonder a wildcat ain't caught it."

"No reason to let that happen," Ike said, shaking out a loop in his rope. "Let's see if me and you can get her, Cal."

Dang thought James as he hung back with the rest, *this isn't the time to be doing this.* Yet, at the same moment, he wished a little rustling was all there was to worry over. He had come out on the wrong side of the law before, but over nothing as drastic as what was in mind for Tom Cooper.

Ike and Cal went toward the mare at a trot, lariats dangling. The sorrel raised her head, ears pricked, and watched the two strangers approaching. When they were within twenty-five feet, she stamped her foot and wheeled for the safety of the brush. The men popped spurs to their mounts and burst forth.

Cal was enthusiastic and jockeyed his horse up to her right side, but his whirling loop was off target and struck the side of her head. A snort came from the fleeing animal as she angled left. The bay made the cut quickly, never losing speed, and Ike's rope snaked out to fall around the mare's neck.

After she was under control and calmed, Ike led her up to the others. Sun glistened on her flanks and even Dirk and James were pleased with her appearance. However, the latter remarked, "Now, if we ain't all dead when this is over, maybe she'll pay for this trip."

Bill admonished, "Don't worry so much, Cousin. Just be ready when the trouble does start."

James told himself he was, but he was far from being comfortable when Cal picked up Cooper's sign skirting the baygall behind the smokehouse. Older, un-shod tracks were now visible in spots.

"We're on the right track," Ike said from where they were milling over the sign. It was getting late, and the horses were tired. He didn't plan to go much further, the memory of what had happened the evening before still fresh. "Let's ride single file and keep some distance between us. That way we won't be such a bunched-up target."

"Yeah," Dirk thought aloud, "and the one in the lead will be the first to get his guts blown out."

Ike frowned at Dirk and grunted, then flipped him the sorrel's lead rope. Drawing his Henry from its scabbard, he led the way himself.

Either Cooper or Stan kept watch on their back trail for several hundred yards at all times. Peters, able to stand with the crutch, gathered some cane to make fishing poles with the little line and few hooks they had. Martha and Belle helped him set them along the creek bank in hopes of picking up some catfish during the warming trend.

The camp itself was situated a few yards back from the creek in a hollow of black gums and hollies, and over a mile northeast of the prior one. Tom planned for him and Stan to take turns keeping watch during the night, unless it wouldn't be needed after he followed through with his plan.

With several hours of work, a crude sleeping shelter was made for the Peters family under the largest holly. By cutting and placing yaupons between and among the lower branches, a crude roof was made in case of rain. Beds of pine boughs were laid beneath, and a similar structure was set up for Waters and Tom nearby.

It was the middle of the afternoon before the work was completed and a small meal prepared. After eating, Tom finished his second cup of coffee by the fire and surveyed the camp. It was time to divulge his thoughts and take some action.

He rose to his feet. "We've got it set up pretty good. I'm going to ride back to the other campsite and see if they do follow me. I believe they will, and I want to be waiting on them."

Tom and Belle had been unable to say very much to one another, but she did seem just as friendly as before, and her frequent smile was warm. Now she looked up at him with definite concern. "What will you do?" she asked.

The look on the young man's face bothered Shane, as it had Stan upon relating about the burning of the farm, and the old man commented seriously, "That's a lot of men for one man to face."

Belle realized that Tom meant to stand and fight, and the thought terrified her. "You can't. They . . . there's too many for you alone."

Tom's right hand was resting on the grip of his tied-down Colt, and he looked down at her upturned face. He could see it for sure now—she cared for him more than just a friend. How much more, he did not know, but her full lips seemed to tremble.

"You won't be alone." It was the Caddo who made the remark.

Turning, Cooper said, "You've been hurt on my account, too. I'll wait for them till dark, maybe longer.

If they are still after me, they'll eventually show up there.

"It's me they want. I don't want anyone taking any more risks for me. This time, if there's any running done, they'll be the ones to do it."

Stan Waters slung the quiver and bow over his lean shoulder as if Tom hadn't said a word. "You wouldn't deny a man the chance to repay a debt, would you?" He pointed to his temple, the bandage now removed, his black hair hanging freely, and a smile softened his hard facial features. "That Ike Landis gave me a good headache. I want to give him somethin'."

Tom nodded assent with a half-grin, there was nothing else he could do, and mounted his black. For lack of knowing what to say, he only touched his hat in Belle's direction before riding away with the Indian.

Shane warned them to be careful and Martha murmured a prayer, but Belle could say nothing; her eyes were moist, and she feared her voice would tremble. She wondered if she had made a fool of herself. Not able to even look her parents in the eye, she stood and began washing the few cooking and eating utensils, of which most came from Tom's own gear.

Did he even care for her a little? Would he and Stan return? She couldn't be sure of the answer to either question.

The two's horses were hidden well away from the opening at the bottom of the ridge. Tom and Stan were concealed in the shadows of some chaparral behind a red oak with a good view of the former encampment.

With the day waning the air was cooling, and Tom was wearing his duster again. They had been there for over an hour, and he'd repeatedly warned the Indian to cut and run should things get bad. But Stan would always change the subject to strategy, and Tom wasn't sure his words had any effect.

He took a deep breath and whispered, "How far will that bow shoot?"

"Not very accurate past the other side of the clearing." Stan's voice, as always, was amazingly soft and smooth.

Tom craved a cigarette and shifted his position to get his mind off of the habit. The flare of a match, smell of smoke, or the glowing of the tip when he dragged would all do well in advertising their presence in the evening shadows.

All was calm for a while. Then suddenly the sounds of approaching riders drifted across the clearing. Tom saw Waters moving off to the right, nocking an arrow. He hoped the Caddo would heed his warnings.

An icy trickle of sweat ran down Tom's neck and his palms became damp as Ike rode into view. The man was bold. Seconds ticked by and the other four came in sight one at a time. Dirk had Shane's red sorrel in tow, and they all halted, long guns resting on their thighs. Ike Landis was ahead, examining the ashes of the campfire. Bill began moving up to him, and Cooper stepped into view, Spencer planted firmly against his shoulder.

"Drop those rifles!" he commanded, aiming at the center of the big man's torso. The horses shied a little at his appearance and voice, and all the men quickly obeyed. All except the one in Tom's sights.

"You sneaky—"

Cooper interrupted him, "We can chat after you're unarmed! Now drop your rifle, Ike, and all of you unbuckle your gunbelts. You started this, but I can finish it if I have to. I mean it!"

Bill's hand was dangerously close to his six-gun, and Ike's fingers were white from the grip on his Henry. No one made a move for their belt buckles save James and Dirk, and Cooper's gaze flickered to them. Then their motions were stopped abruptly by Ike's hasty decision.

"Darn you!" he bellowed, crouching low in the saddle and trying to jerk the repeater's muzzle up.

Chapter Nine

The quick movement of the bay's master made it sling its head, thus saving the man's life. Cooper's shot from the Spencer hit the animal and it collapsed like a giant tree beneath Ike Landis, throwing his shot twelve feet short of Tom. Ike then lost his weapon as he hurled himself away from the crushing weight of the beast.

Bill's hand had just closed on the butt of his revolver when an arrow sank into the fleshy part of his left shoulder. Instead of finishing the draw, he wheeled his horse and retreated for the line of brush and trees, shouting, "That Injun's with him!"

The remaining three's play was made in a flash. Their pistols began barking as their horses danced in fright. Dirk headed back with Bill, the sorrel's lead rope in his left hand with his reins, his right hand hurling lead. Crawfishing back to the red oak, Tom began working the action of the carbine. Only one of his slugs found a mark.

Cal was the last to fall back to the safety of the timber, and his bravado was paid with a gash cut into his cheek by one of the huge .56 caliber balls. An arrow grazed the rump of his horse as it charged through the brush.

Tom peeked from around his nature-made shield when the volley of bullets stopped hammering the bark. Ike was in a prone position at the belly of his dead horse, only the width of its body for cover, and was triggering his pistol over it. Though Tom knew the power of the Spencer was not likely to penetrate the saddle and depth of the dead mount to reach the man, he levered the last two shots from the magazine at it in frustration.

A thump sounded as one of Stan's missiles imbedded in the same target, and then a hiss as another disappeared into the brush where the other men were figured to be. The twin cracks of six-guns came in answer, and Tom returned them with two of his own before Ike forced him back behind the tree. Muzzle flashes and noise were the only things to shoot at in the dark brush—night was moving in fast—and he heard some scrambling in the thicket but wasn't sure he'd scored a hit, or just come close.

"Pin 'em down!" Ike bawled from his cramped position. He was mad, and a little worried.

Tom waited for Ike Landis to make a run for the

thicket. Things were different now, he had given them a chance and he meant to kill. It was quiet for only a moment.

Projectiles of lead bombarded his shield, the air, and ground around him, and he knew this was it. He jumped up and crabbed quickly to his right, fanning the Colt at waist level, with the bottom of his duster billowing out from his body at the movement. The fleeing Landis was almost to the trees.

Ike's revolver was empty and he concentrated on running fast and low for the brush. His companions were sending a turbulent hail of covering fire, but he heard one slug buzz close by, and two more rattled into the twigs of the dense growth ahead. Just as he made a lunge for the depths of the thicket something tore at his leg. Only a nick from an arrow. He reached Bill and the rest and they began a full-scale retreat.

Tom Cooper leaned against another tree, scanning the battlefield and reloading his pistol. Silence shrouded the scene except for the pounding hoofbeats of the enemies' horses. By the time Tom pushed the sixth .44 cartridge home, that too had dispersed. He swore. Would they give it up now?

"You okay, Stan?"

"Not a scratch." The words came so near in the darkness of the timber that Tom flinched. The Caddo's form emerged and he motioned to the lower part of Cooper's duster. "A bow don't give off a flash when it shoots."

Tom stepped further into the light of the clearing to examine the tail of his duster. On the left side there were two black-rimmed, dime-sized holes punched through the material, and he didn't have to be told that they weren't made by moths.

"Looks like they lost the nerve for fightin' once we got the upper hand," Stan remarked, standing beside him in the dim light. "Weakened 'em a good deal."

Tom looked from the dead horse to the strewn rifles. He moved forward to gather them. "I appreciate your help. Bill would have probably taken me out if you hadn't put that arrow in him."

Stan began to help pick up the weapons. "We won this battle, but they still may not quit. That Ike is a bad one," he said.

Of all four rifles, Ike's was the only repeater. It had been a good victory, and Tom, having just fought for his life, thought of his days on the battlefields in the war. Like that, this fighting was ridiculous, and he prayed Ike would stop.

In Ike's saddlebags they found only a very little jerky, a tin cup and plate, part of a box of .44's, and a broken bottle of whiskey, the contents of which had thoroughly soaked a pair of clothing. A worn poncho and bedroll were lashed behind the cantle, and Tom seized them to increase the quality of their own camp. Stan retrieved an arrow from the ground that wasn't damaged and led the way back from the ground that wasn't damaged and led the way back to their mustangs. It was a deathly still night, yet not very cold.

"Maybe we've clipped their wings," Tom speculated on the way to the camp.

Stan's voice wafted ominously through the dark. "I

don't know. I've seen many men, and those of Ike's nature usually don't take defeat well. Counting the mare they stole, they still have enough mounts. We'll have to see what happens."

The hate Tom had seen in the big man's face as he held the Spencer on him would not subside in a hurry. Tom digested this fact until they were met not by the Peterses and their stocky dog at the camp.

"Are you all right?" Belle asked quickly.

"Thank God," Martha said after the duo's affirmation.

"We could hear the shootin'," Peters said. He sat a little way from the small fire, his muzzleloader close by. At the sight of all the loot, he asked, "What happened?"

Stan hobbled the horses while Tom told the story. Martha and Belle fixed supper as they listened, and he chose his words carefully for their benefit.

Shane summed it up with, "Sounds like it was some fight. It's a wonder nobody was killed." He spat after a minute. "I agree with Stan, though. I don't look fer 'em to give it up now. Unless they have a mighty big change of heart."

Thanks to Stan there was plenty of fried corn bread and sweet potatoes for the meal. Only one catfish was caught on Shane's bank poles, but it helped out. The critters didn't bite much that time of year the old farmer explained.

Conversation was somber during the meal, mainly concerning the events of the previous days, the guard they would keep posted at night, and their dwindling meat supply. They decided Stan and Tom would slip back to the smokehouse the next morning for some more of the cured pork and venison, after waiting a while to make sure the Landises wouldn't try an early attack—if one at all.

Tom insisted on taking the first watch and, when the camp settled for the night, sat down under a low-branched holly outside the perimeter of the clearing. The heavy foliage of the evergreen shrouded him in almost total darkness. In less than a half-hour, light footsteps neared him.

He was about to stand when a whisper came. "Tom? Tom, where are you?" It was Belle, and he couldn't bring himself to chastise the young woman for disturbing his sentry duty.

"Right here," he replied, whispering. What would her parents think of her joining him *alone* at that time of night? "What is it?"

"I . . . I couldn't sleep. Just wanted to talk, I'm sorry."

"Don't be. Sit down if you want." He was nervous because it was his first chance to talk to her alone, but his voice was confident. At least he hoped it was. She stooped under the limbs of the tree and sat next to him. Her hand touched his arm as she did, and a warmness settled over Tom. "Why couldn't you sleep?" he asked.

"Worried, I guess." There was a pause. "Those men are horrible."

"I'm really sorry about all this. I wish—"

"No. It isn't your fault. I'm just scared for Pa and

Ma—and you. And Stan, he's always been so good to us." She said the last hurriedly, and Tom thought he detected a tremor in her words.

"He's being a great friend by helping me too." There was an awkward silence. "Are you cold?"

Belle moved a little. "No, I have on one of the buckskin shirts Stan brought us for jackets."

"I hope they'll leave you alone." Her hand was suddenly on his arm again. She squeezed it gently and concluded before rising, "I better get back to bed."

"Good night," was the only thing Tom said as she walked away, and he felt foolish for it. He should have said something else. But what?

He spent the remainder of his guard duty thinking about the girl and her short visit. She had nothing more than her shoes, blue cotton dress, and a shirt of deerskin to wear; nothing more than a bed of pine boughs and old blankets out in the elements to sleep on. And it was his fault.

The night for the Landises was pure hell. Their camp, if it could be called one, was across the wagon road, three miles southwest from the scene of the fight. At the present, Dirk and James were working to get the arrow out of Bill's shoulder while Cal and Ike tended their own minor wounds. Luckily the arrow had missed any bones, but the pain was causing its victim to spew the air with profane oaths as Dirk snapped off the feathered end of the shaft and pushed the head on through. Pulling it out had proved impossible.

When it was completely extracted Bill took a long swig from the bottle of sour mash that was clutched in his hand. He expelled air through his teeth as he poured a liberal portion into the raw hole. James quickly bandaged it.

After the terrible burning of the alcohol in the wound had subsided, Bill leaned back against his saddle at the head of his blankets and breathed deeply. "That Indian's gonna pay."

James scowled but said nothing and went to the fire. Dirk, however, exploded, "Ike! You could've gotten us all killed with that crazy move!"

Cal's cheek finally stopped bleeding and he drained the next to the last bottle of whiskey. "I'm sick of your whinin'," he growled. "You didn't get a scratch and you're carryin' on like a baby. Why don't you lay off?"

Dirk's temper rose, but he didn't have a chance for a rebuttal before Ike added, "You know, I got enough to worry about without listening to your complaining all the time. Cooper just killed the best horse I ever owned. My change of clothes was with all my other gear. And now he's got my Henry rifle!"

James finally spoke. "He got my Sharps, too. All any of us has got is our pistols. But that ain't the point! What about Bill's shoulder gettin' infected?"

"I was hurt worse than this at Baton Rouge," Bill said. "Laid up for three months with busted ribs from a Yankee's musket ball. This ain't affected my gun arm. And I can get around." He was steadily emptying the last quart of liquor.

Dirk turned to the wounded man. "Why can't y'all see it? Cooper is good, and now he's hooked up with an Indian that's just as good."

"We've done our share of fightin'—regrettably on both sides of the law—but I want y'all to know I am against this," James said, his tone low.

Ike thumped his half-smoked cigarette at their pitiful excuse for a fire. "I'd say you've both made that awful clear. Go on home. Me, Cal, and Bill will be there soon as its over, even if that means goin' through that Indian."

A minute of silence passed, Dirk and James both giving it considerable thought, then Cal declared, "Poor Randy would roll over in his grave if he knew you were backin' out! Not to mention Pa! Don't y'all have any guts?"

Dirk felt like shaking his little brother. "Pa would have agreed with us and you know it! I loved Randy just as much as any of you. But killin' Cooper won't bring Randy back!"

"Make me feel a mite better," Ike stated.

"Aw, let 'em go," Cal advised the big man with a smirk. "They're yellow!"

Dirk practically screamed, "You damn young fool! We should have stopped Randy! He was drunk and didn't know what he was gettin' into! You think you're bad, but if that guy's bullet had been two inches to your right, you'd have ended up just like him! That what you want?"

Even by the dim firelight all could see Cal's face darken. He came to his feet and stepped menacingly toward Dirk, preparing to strike out. James jumped up, caught the young man by the arm, and swung him roughly around. "Stop it! It isn't a time to be fighting amongst ourselves!"

"You don't want to fight nobody," Cal retorted.

James reflected on the truth in those words. He should ride out, but would not, and said as much. "I'm not speakin' for Dirk. He can do what he feels he ought. And I sure won't hold it agin him if he leaves right now. We all should."

Four pairs of eyes gazed at Dirk and he felt a terrific weight settle on his chest. He wished that they would all head back with him to Louisiana, but the looks on their faces showed further discussion would only bring about more trouble. And leaving them behind was something he just couldn't make himself do. His fingers played absently over the butt of his revolver, tied low on his hip.

"I ain't gonna leave you all behind to get killed. But we'd better start plannin' what to do," he said simply and went to unroll his blankets.

Ike curled up in two of the other men's ponchos a few feet from the dying embers. He was glad for the quiet. His stomach growled at the small amount of jerky and whiskey he'd consumed. "We sure as hell need some grub. We'll decide what to do come mornin'," he asserted.

James sat up for a long time in the shadows, nursing a faint hope that Ike's decision to continue the quest might somehow change by daylight.

* * *

Over two hours of anxious waiting and watching followed the dawn light. Tom and Stan kept circling the camp at a distance, and once backtracked to the scene of the battle to make sure that the Landises weren't trying to locate them. Wolves had found the bay's carcass during cover of darkness, and now buzzards were taking their share of the remains. Having not seen anything of the vengeful men, Tom's hopes grew as he and Stan left for the smokehouse.

Belle stood watching and listening as they disappeared into the woods. Three of the rifles had been left with them, and Tom had said to keep them handy. Her father was resting with the Henry in his arms and his flintlock nearby. Stan was carrying the Sharps carbine with him in addition to his bow, and the remaining two lay in reach of Martha.

Belle had unconsciously walked to the clearing's edge, near the place where she and Tom had talked privately the previous night, and was staring unseeingly in the direction the handsome man had gone. She reflected on the reason why she'd sought him out for conversation. What had she really wanted to tell him? He had made no move toward her that would indicate he cared for her in any way more than just wanting to help her family.

Her mother was suddenly beside her, hand on her shoulder. "You love him, don't you?"

The older woman's question caught her by surprise. Belle looked into her knowing face, then glanced to her father across the opening. He was obviously busy with his own thoughts, but her voice was low as she answered, "I . . . I think maybe yes. But I've only known him for such a short time."

Martha smiled. "Things happen fast in a country like this, and he's a good man, no doubt, or he wouldn't be jeopardizing himself to help us. But sometimes men like him don't stay in one place long. He may ride on after the farm is rebuilt."

Belle had already given that some thought even though she didn't have much experience with men. "I know, Ma," she said. "I'll just have to wait and see."

Martha hugged her daughter with one arm and went back to where Shane was poking sticks to the fire. Belle looked at the wintery forest once again before joining her parents and concluded to herself, *Yes, I'll just have to wait and see.*

Tom and Stan left their mounts hitched to a post of the shed at the back of the smokehouse and hurried in to renew their supply of meat. The sun was shining brightly and birds were singing. The building smelled of rich oak and hickory smoke, and Cooper enjoyed the odors while placing several strips of jerked venison and a smoked-pork ham in a cloth sack.

Stan started a small fire under the remaining meat, which hung from poles across the ceiling, to make sure it stayed cured, saying that they could come back and add more wood later. He picked up a little keg of salt for cooking and exited behind Tom.

There wasn't much talk, and they headed back to the horses, walking shoulder to shoulder. A metallic click that made the hair rise on Tom's neck halted them before they turned the corner. It came from behind, and he'd heard the noise too many times to mistake it.

Chapter Ten

Waters stiffened, the grip on the rifle tightening, and Cooper's free hand eased closer to his pistol. "Y'all just let them weapons fall and turn around slow." The words sounded forceful enough, especially since the two men didn't know exactly how many of the enemy they faced, and they followed the command.

After unfastening his gunbelt one handedly, Tom turned to face their captor: only one, and the youngest of the bunch, Cal Landis. For a moment Tom wished he'd tried something, but instantly knew he would have died. But now what? The kid was standing six feet away grinning triumphantly. There was no cover, so he had obviously slipped up while they were inside and stepped from around the corner of the building.

117

"Well, it looks like I got you!"

Stan questioned, "Where are the others?"

"At camp. This was just luck. Looks like I was sent here for the same reason y'all came. But, hey, dead men don't need to worry about eatin.' " Cal was jubilant. He couldn't wait to show Ike these two men's corpses.

Tom saw the glint in the young man's eyes and knew they needed time. His Colt lay at his feet and Stan was void of rifle and bow. Yet the sack of meat was still in Tom's left hand.

What he needed was for Cal to make a mistake.

"After the whipping we gave you last night," he goaded, "I figured y'all would be limping back to whatever hole it was you crawled out of."

"You talk pretty tough. Myself, I don't feel like chatting," Cal said calmly. "I was taught to never trust an Indian. So I'm gonna kill him first."

Tom opened his mouth to speak, but Landis stepped nearer and leveled the cocked revolver at arm's length in the Caddo's hard, unflinching face, and he knew it was beyond talking. It was time for acting.

Estimating the shortened distance between himself and the death-dealing weapon, Tom hurled the bag of meat at Cal's hand, just as his finger began to squeeze the trigger. The pistol vomited flame and the ball whistled by Stan's head. Tom rushed in low, his shoulder connecting solidly with Cal's stomach. Both men went to the ground in a tangle, the gun lost in the fall.

Stan stepped forward to give assistance, but Tom was already jerking the young man to his feet by the collar of his coat, and he said, "No. If he wants me, let him see if he can take me!" As soon as the words were spat out Tom knocked his opponent away with a right to the jaw.

The Caddo took a position by the fallen weapons and watched the two men meet toe to toe. He could understand Tom's desire to handle this tight fight himself.

Cal Landis only backpedalled from Cooper's first punch and came in readily. They exchanged a barrage of blows in which the wound on Cal's cheek was reopened. It bled down his face and onto his clothing. Tom took a good shot to the chin and realized that although Cal was younger and lighter he was no stranger to a brawl. Tom managed to pummel Cal to the ground; Cal rolled once on the side of the little knoll and practically bounced back to his feet.

Tom was ready, his breathing deep and rapid, and he worked the kid further toward the ruined cabin with combinations to the body and head. Cal hit the dirt again and was slower in rising, but this time steel flashed in the sunlight. The knife had a five inch blade and made its appearance from his boot. Tom dodged a slash and backed up a step.

"Come on now, Yankee!" Cal taunted with the knife outstretched between them.

Knowing better than to rush in—that was exactly what his opponent wanted—Tom crouched and started to circle. Time would pass and break the other man's nerve. And it did.

Cal was filled with rage. He snarled like an animal

and finally made a cut for the eyes. Tom ducked and grabbed his wrist before he could make a backslash. A howl of pain erupted from the knife's wielder as Tom wrenched it away and forced him to the earth. Tom held him by the collar and pressed the point of the knife against Cal's throat until a spot of crimson showed. The pinned man stopped struggling, breath coming in gasps.

Boiling anger made Tom want to sink the knife to its haft. But he couldn't. "Dang it, boy!" he bellowed. "I ought to cut your head off!"

Cal looked defiant, just a trace of fear. "Why not? Might as well kill me like you did Randy!"

Tom's voice was hard. "That wasn't my fault. The kid made that decision himself. You and your clan have caused enough havoc for me and the Peterses! Look at those burned buildings!

"Now listen close. You're going to take a message back to the others. If you cause any more trouble for us—even come in sight—I'll kill every damn one of you. I swear it!"

Jerking the young man up, he shoved him away. "Get out of here!"

Landis glared at him before walking over to pick up his hat. His brain burned with hatred and he could hardly swallow the humiliation. The Indian, now fully armed, stepped between him and his revolver.

"You ride without a gun," Stan said. "Get your horse and go." Cal clenched his bruised fists and marched toward the baygall. Pounding hooves soon diminished to the south.

With the very real possibility of the gunshot bringing the rest, if they were in hearing distance, Tom and Stan hurried to get away. They chose not to take time to pack along any firewood; they could make do with deadfall for now. Neither spoke for a while.

"We might have been safer if I had killed him," Tom said.

Stan quickly asserted, "You did the right thing. It would have been murder. They will be the ones responsible if it comes to more killing."

Tom rode on and examined the pistol they had captured from Cal, the knife now stored in his saddlebags. Five of the chambers were fully charged in the old gun. The thought of the time it took to load cap-and-ball revolvers made him glad he'd had his Colt Army converted to handle metal cartridges. His inspection and thoughts were broken by Stan.

"You are a fine taysha."

A puzzled frown creased Tom's brow. "A what?"

"*Taysha*. It's what my father's people called other tribes of the Caddo confederacies. It means friend or ally. If not for you, I'd be dead now."

"I didn't do anything for you that you wouldn't have done for me. You've stuck your neck out to help me. I'd say we're even."

"Still, I owe you, and will not forget."

To break the somber mood Tom Cooper handed the Colt Dragoon over to his friend. "It hasn't got but five shots and I don't have any supplies to load it. But it'll throw some lead. You know how to use it?"

Waters nodded in affirmation as he took the gun.

He slid it beneath his beaverskin belt and said, "Thanks. We probably haven't seen the last of them yet."

No matter how he hoped they had, Tom could not convince himself of it. Cal had been stripped of all his weapons, and, as far as he knew, the others only had six-guns—and their hate. The last could be enough to keep them coming.

But he and Stan were very well armed and hopefully they could take care of anything that might arise. A serious problem was the fact that their own group had only two mounts. The mules would need to be found. For the lack of grain and chances to forage, the mustangs were a little thin. Yet Tom wasn't worried, for they were the toughest kind of horses because of their natural ability to survive during harsh situations. His black had been caught somewhere along the Brazos and brought to Louisiana for sale. Tom was still pleased with his purchase.

Martha took the meat and Belle fussed over a slight cut over Tom's left eye which he'd received in the fight. Everyone was astounded at their story. Tom couldn't help but enjoy the attention Belle was giving his minor wound, and he felt the need to talk with her alone again, but Shane's sad statement brought him back to what was most important.

"There's a bit of cold weather left, but it ain't long 'til spring. If we don't stop fightin' and get to rebuilding the farm, I won't be able to get a crop in."

After mulling the situation over while the rest talked, Tom proposed, "Why don't we just sit tight as possible for a couple days? Me and Stan can take turns looking for the lost mules, and it will give us time to see if they're going to leave us be. If they do, I'll go into town and get some things we're going to need for the work."

They didn't feel especially hopeful, but there was always a chance, and they agreed. Things were very quiet over the noon meal.

Ike became enraged as Cal told of his run-in with Cooper and the Indian. He began to pace to release some energy, a plan starting to form in the back of his mind, still vague yet. "James, I want you and Dirk to scout for their camp. Hide your horses close to where we had the scrap last night and go in on foot. I don't want 'em tipped off. Best wait closer to dark. Don't try nothin', just see where they're at.

"Cal, you take this"—he handed over his gunbelt—"and go south. Try to get some game. Jerky's about gone."

The youngest Landis left immediately on the chore. Dirk and James digested their assignment for once without a word and lounged around to await evening. Bill's shoulder showed no sign of infection and he was resting. Ike waited anxiously. He would relate the other part of his idea later.

"I'm going to get more wood," Belle announced, rising from beside the fire.

Peters looked at the darkening sky. "You don't need to be off by yourself," he said, trying to stand. "I'll go. Tom and Stan have been ridin' after them mules all afternoon."

Belle objected, "Pa, your leg isn't well enough to be carrying firewood. You barely managed to set those bank poles yesterday. I won't go far. I just want to walk a bit."

Tom had to keep himself from appearing too eager as he offered, "I'll go with her. If you don't mind."

Shane looked at him then Belle. "Feel better if you're along. Go ahead," he consented.

The two went to the creek and along its edge in silence, picking up little twigs and limbs, anything that would create heat. The night was closing in with a damp chill. She was the first to speak.

"Do you think we'll get them back, Pa's mules?"

"It's doubtful, but maybe." Upon first meeting her, Tom had felt so at ease. Now, since his feelings had grown for her, he couldn't think of any small talk.

There was another stretch of time that passed before she said, "I know you're tired, after riding all evening."

"Never too tired to walk with a pretty girl. Even under these circumstances." It was the first romantic thing he had said to her and hoped he hadn't messed up. He thought he saw her blush, but it was hard to tell in the shadows.

Her laugh was soft and light. "Pretty?" She motioned to her disarrayed clothing. "I must be a sight."

He stooped to pick up a pine knot and said evenly, "You are. A beautiful one."

She halted and turned toward him, her eyes big and

brown. Tom felt like a schoolboy as he looked at her upturned face, and suddenly he knew what he'd been wanting to say to her. Instead, he leaned forward and kissed her gently on the lips, their small bundles of twigs rustling between them. She did not back away as he feared.

Seconds ticked by, uncomfortable and magnificent at the same time, as they stared at one another. Their breath made fog in the cold air. He finally turned and looked around anxiously, then went to the water's edge. A large willow limb had fallen half into the creek, and handing what small amount of kindling he'd found to Belle, Tom picked it up and slung it over his left shoulder with a grunt. The wet end dripped behind.

"I think we've just about got all the little stuff," he declared. "Let's get back. Maybe this will last most of the night, after it dries out."

She fell in beside him, and they said little. He walked with his right arm around her until right before entering camp. He just didn't have enough nerve now to tell her that he loved her. Maybe later. Sometime soon.

A norther, accompanied by sleet, had blown in during the night. An hour of daylight passed and, although the sleeting stopped, ice cloaked the ground. The fire crackled under a cottontail Cal had killed right after dawn. Ike watched as some juices dripped from the meat and concluded that it was time to tell what he had in mind. James and Dirk had had exceptionally good luck in their scouting expedition of the evening before—they'd even gotten close enough to see an intimate moment between Cooper and the farmer's girl at the creek. Ike filed this way for further consideration later, and now he felt it was just a matter of time.

"Cal, saddle your, James, and Bill's horses," he ordered. "Dirk, we're gonna leave what little beef jerky we've got with you and Bill. I want all of us to pool our money." He motioned to the other two. "We're goin' to town."

"What for?" came the return.

Eyeing Dirk like a child, Ike said, "Because we're in bad need of supplies. Can't you tell? Since we know where they are, once we get outfitted again, we can finish Cooper off quick."

Dirk grunted, barely audible, and tossed his money into the little pile from the others' pockets. Ike counted it while Cal and James finished readying the horses and was pleased with the total. He shoved it into his trousers and said, "I'm taking the mare to get some gear for her." At Dirk's frown, he added, "Y'all just sit tight. You won't need to be ridin' unless your hunting meat. I want to ride Bill's horse so it won't look so funny me goin' in bareback."

Hunkered by the fire, wounded shoulder bandaged heavily and his arm resting on his knee, Bill commented, "Give me a little time to rest up, anyhow. Be careful, and bring back a bottle of redeye."

Dirk said, "There's a lot we need, and that ain't an awful lot of money."

Ike stepped into the leather and started northwest to

hit the wagon road a short distance away, towing the sorrel behind. "We'll make it do. Be back in a day or two."

The forest was deathly quiet and the four mounts seemed to make a deafening racket in the cold, still surroundings, even when they were on the rutted trail. When the road finally veered due north; the men snugged the ragged collars of their wool-lined coats tighter and bowed their heads to the oncoming wind.

Chapter Eleven

The cold morning was miserable, yet Tom Cooper knew the tracks were fresh because of the night's precipitation, and so he was grateful. He'd been zigzagging through thickets along the creek and river for two hours without seeing any sign of the mules or the cow. Now, within ten minutes of finding the prints, he came in sight of one of the mules standing placidly in a pin oak flat.

Its long ears flickered as Cooper eased his mustang forward with a rope, yet it made no attempt to bolt when he flipped the loop neatly over its head. The stillness of the morning had kept Tom somewhat unnerved, an ever-present fear of one of the Landises popping up. However, his group now had another mount, and he started back for the camp, breathing lighter as his thoughts centered again on Belle.

He did love the young woman, and that was a first in his life. Sure, there had been some others that he had been close to, plenty he'd known much longer than Belle, but it wasn't the same as this. She hadn't backed away from his advances, and that added to his wanting to tell her his feelings. It had happened awfully fast, but he couldn't deny that he wanted her and a place to put down roots.

"I'll be danged!" Peters exclaimed upon seeing his mule. "I'm glad you found him."

Waters took the lead rope and said, "I was about to give up on finding any of 'em. Any sign of trouble?"

"None. Maybe they took what I told Cal to heart." Tom took a piece of ham and a sweet potato that Belle offered him, and his heart leaped. There was that smile that came not only from the lips, but from down deep in her brown eyes. He eventually managed to say, "If nothing happens soon, I need to make that trip to Maple Springs. By selling these extra rifles we can get a good start at buying some of the stuff that was lost."

Stan hobbled the mule and stated, "You've been riding a good while. I'll make a round now. Was there any sign that the other one might be close by where you found this fella?"

Tom extended his hands to the fire and shook his head. "His was the first and only tracks I've seen."

Sitting around the flames with the Peterses was relaxing in spite of the dampness. Shane was extremely happy over the recovery of his animal, though still very much concerned over the work that lay in the future months. They talked a little of the supplies that were a definite must for the construction of the barn and house. Tom was eager to get a start, and neither he nor Stan had found evidence that the Landises were lurking nearby.

Around midday Shane got to his feet. He was able to walk much better than was expected, his leg showing every sign of healing quickly. "I'm gonna see if I can find more wood. This cold spell is hangin' on real good, and tonight's lookin' to be pretty nippy."

"I'll go," Tom proposed.

"Thanks, but what this leg needs is some exercise. Sitting around here will make an old man out at me sure enough."

"I'll go with you," Martha said.

The insistent look on his wife's face and the sound in her voice told Shane there was no use objecting. Also, he figured she might want to talk to him alone; there had been a peculiar glimmer in her eyes when she looked at Belle and Tom lately. He adjusted one of the buckskin shirts over his own and said to Tom, "We'll come get you if we find something too big for us to tote."

Cooper nodded and watched the couple walk away. Belle added a pine knot to the fire and stirred it up. Tom looked on in silence, the weight of another moment alone with her heavy on his mind. He wanted to say what needed saying. But how should he begin?

"I can hardly wait till spring," she said.

"Isn't long off. It's my favorite time of year."

"Really? Mine too. Everything's so green and fresh, like a whole new beginning to life."

"You have a way with words." He envied her for it at present.

"Not really." She laughed and sat near him. They talked of the weather and the problems they faced, but neither mentioned the night before or their kiss. However, Tom seemed to be wanting to say something, and the wondering at what it was made Belle more nervous. She hoped it was what she wanted to hear.

Tom decided he was wasting time. Shane and Martha would be back soon. He had to get it off his chest, just in case something were to happen to him. Her dress was showing wear, as was his own clothing, and her hair wasn't as kempt as it had been the day they met, but there was no hiding the beauty that came from deep within.

"Belle, I realize this is kind of fast—I mean, there hasn't been a chance for what you call courting—and last night I . . ."

Her breath caught at his abrupt pause. *He's finally going to say whatever it is,* she thought. He was searching for the words, and she wanted to make it easier for him, even if he was going to say that their kiss was a mistake. But that didn't seem the case. Her face became warm and she looked away.

"I've never done much of that, anyway. Us living so far from town and all. As you see, we don't have many neighbors, and there isn't anything to do but picnic."

Her calmness made him feel better. He waved his hand at the surroundings. "Well, we've done a lot of that."

She laughed again and his confidence grew. He blurted, "I love you, Belle. And I'd like to have you for my wife." He wanted to believe the sudden expression on her face was happiness instead of shock. Picking up her hand, he added, "You don't have to say anything now. I don't know how strongly you feel about me, but I want to be sure this trouble with the Landises is over."

Belle didn't have to think. "Ma said things happen fast, sometimes," she returned. "I'll give you my answer now. I think you will make me a wonderful husband."

The words were almost as beautiful as the person who said them. It was the greatest minute of Tom's life. He took her in his arms and kissed her like he'd wanted to for so long, then held her close and speculated, "It's been awhile since I've done any farming, but there's a lot of free land around here, and it's as good a time as any to start back." They kissed again, and Tom knew he'd found a permanent home in East Texas.

Stan returned right ahead of Shane and Martha. He had met them on their hunt for firewood and was dragging a small pine log. The elderly couple each carried an armload of kindling. Belle and Tom had decided to wait until after he made the trip to town to tell of their engagement.

"Found the cow dead three miles north of here,"

came the Indian's report. "Wasn't much left. I'd say a panther."

"I reckon the same went with the other half of my mule team," Peters said glumly.

While supper was being prepared, Tom laid forth a plan. "I'm going to Maple Springs tomorrow unless there's some indication we're going to have more trouble from the Landises. I think they would've already attempted something if they intended to keep after me. Just the same, Stan, me and you can go and get some more meat and wood from the smokehouse early in the morning. We'll do some scoutin' on the way.

"With a store of food and wood, you won't have to go no further than the creek for water, and you can stay around camp with them. I should get back early the next day."

The Caddo grunted in agreement. "Fine. We still need to be careful, and I never was fond of a trip to town."

"I've got some money buried under the shed," Peters announced. He looked to Tom. "It'd help some with the expenses."

"I can cover what we need now, especially after selling the extra rifles," Tom assured him. Stan told him he wanted to keep the Sharps carbine if he could pick up some ammunition for it. Tom said he would and asked Shane, "What kind of mount, if I can find any suitable, do you want to replace that sorrel?"

The old farmer objected, "That's gonna cost plenty, and I don't expect you to pay for all we'll eventually have to have to rebuild. I don't have *much* money, but I want to help pay."

"I know, and you will." Tom grinned. "Don't get me wrong, I'm not rich. But I do have some saved, and there'll be other trips for supplies. This is just a quick one." His eyes couldn't help but flicker to Belle. "Besides, this is a good investment. Now, what about that horse?"

Peters's eyes watered with appreciation. Then he chuckled. "You're the first fella I've seen in a long time—exceptin' Stan, here—that would use up all his hard-earned money to get an old sodbuster back on his feet." He paused and looked at the hobbled mule. "Well, see if you can buy a mule since we're short one. Broke to ride and plow both, if possible. Like I said earlier, all my tools are under the shed, but you could pick up another double-bit ax."

"And it would be nice to have a plate and cup for everyone to eat out of," his wife added.

Tom laughed. "That it would. We've used our hands enough." For the first time since Bentosa, he felt good.

Maple Springs was quiet on this cold day, not that it was ever very rowdy. Ike and his two brothers rode abreast up the only street, and sloppy mud gouged deep with wagon ruts. Their first destination was the livery, and they pulled up at the gray building. It was a large but simple structure, made for its simple intentions, the last business on the right at the north end of town.

A short, square-shouldered man with a thick red

mustache greeted them just inside the double doors. "Howdy. What can I do fer you?"

James and Cal stood quietly while Ike motioned behind him and explained of his need for gear for the new mare. The hostler glanced out and said, "She's a fine one. Think I got just the thing. Follow me."

He led the way past a forge—he also served as town blacksmith—rows of stalls, a grain box, and under a hayloft to a room at the back right corner of the building. It was evidently a combination living quarters and office; there was a pantry, stove, and a desk and chair on one side, a cot and workbench on the other. A saddle, complete with bags, and a bridle of fair quality hung on the bench, and the man pointed to it with a stubby finger.

"It ain't brand new. Just traded a man for it yesterday. Ya can have the whole outfit for thirty dollars."

Ike said, "I'll take it. Put it on my bill and I'll pay ya when we come to get our horses. And give 'em extra grain. We'll be in town a night or two."

The hostler smiled at getting their business as they headed out and up the boardwalk. James exchanged looks with Cal, both thinking about the total the bill would come to, and the former stared at Ike. Yet he said nothing until they were seated at a secluded table in a saloon, glasses of whiskey and bowls of stew in front of them. This and the hotel cafe were the only places that advertised meals, and naturally they chose the one that also served liquor. Other than the man behind the oak bar, and three men involved in a card game across the room, the establishment was empty.

"Why in hell are we stayin' two nights?" James demanded in a whisper. "And why don't we just camp outside of town?"

Ike forked a piece of boiled beef and said before shoveling it into his mouth, "Might as well take our time. I want that Cooper to get to feeling confident before we go back and finish it. And Dirk and Bill will make out fine."

"How are we going to pay for all we need, plus the horses and our stay?" Cal questioned.

"Long as we don't pay the liveryman, we'll have plenty and some left over."

James frowned at the statement. "And just how you figurin' to get by that?"

"When we get ready to leave, we just tap him on the head, and he won't wake up till we're long gone."

Cal smiled with a mouth full of stew, but James said sarcastically, "Very simple. But what about the law? And somebody might recognize us if we stay that long."

"Not likely," Ike speculated as he leaned forward. "I mean, we ain't been to this hole in the road but maybe four times since the war. And it's been right at five years. As for the law, you forget. Maple Springs ain't got no law." He washed a bite down with a swallow of whiskey, and his smirk indicated he thought his plot amusing.

"Now eat up," he urged. "We'll go over to the general store and buy a couple guns."

That took up a good portion of the afternoon. Ike chose a breech-loading, single-shot rifle, mainly because the price was much less than a repeater. The taking of his Henry made him hate Cooper even more, but he would get his revenge. He felt sure.

James purchased a double-barreled twelve gauge. His heart still wasn't in the fight, but if it must come, he guessed the shotgun might be more effective than the Sharps he lost to Cooper. Especially since the brush was so thick in the area.

Cal, having boosted his confidence even more with several doses of sour mash, took time selecting a pistol that felt just right and fit his holster smoothly. It was a Smith & Wesson .44, and he reflected on how good it would feel to sink one of its slugs into the Yankee.

There weren't enough funds to buy longarms for them all, but they purchased ammunition for Dirk and Bill's belt guns as well as an adequate supply for their own weapons. The three men left the mercantile well-heeled.

Considering the day before, the air was quite warm. Tom Cooper was reassured at finding no sign of the Landises on his and Stan's trip back to the smoke-house. He'd left for town around midmorning, traveling due north through the forest, then angling west until he hit the wagon road. Before his departure he had kissed Belle again, and there had been no objection from her parents. In fact, they seemed to have realized something had taken place between them.

It was now the middle of the afternoon and Tom felt good as he trotted the mustang up to the two-story hotel and acquired a room. He left his bedroll and guns there, then proceeded to the livery stables. Maple Springs wasn't nearly as big as Bentosa. Yet, from the painted signs over the awnings of the businesses, it appeared to have anything the common man would want.

"Got room for another horse tonight?" he queried the stout man who was working on a horseshoe at a forge inside the big doors.

The man knuckled back his red mustache and took the black's reins. "Sure. Anything special fer him?"

"Might check his hooves, and feed him plenty. Been away from oats for awhile.

"I'm interested in buying a mule that's broke to ride and plow. Know of somewhere I can find one?"

The hostler spat tobacco juice and replied, "I got a fairly young one that'll ride. He ain't used to a plow, but it shouldn't be hard to learn him, though."

"Let me see him."

Tom rolled and lit a cigarette while the man put his gelding up and brought out a buckskin mule. He quickly began scanning the animal. He ran his hand along its shoulders, back, and hips in search of any unsoundness. Examining the teeth, Tom saw that the man had been truthful about its age. The mule was strong, but extremely docile, and would make a good match for Shane's gray.

"Got an outfit for him?"

The liveryman spat again and was honest. "Only saddle and bridle I got left is kinda old. I've done some repair work on it, though, and it's got some life left in it. I'll let you have the gear and the mule for forty-five dollars."

"Deal," Tom said, extending his hand. "I'm Tom Cooper. I'll get them when I come to get the mustang in the morning."

"Fine. Name's Shep Barlow. I'll be waitin'."

Cooper carried the three rifles that he had taken from the Landises over to the mercantile wrapped in his blankets. The proprietor, a slim, balding man some twenty years his senior, adjusted his spectacles and looked warily at him when he laid the guns on the counter. "Looks like you won a battle."

The man's words and expression were almost enough to bring a smile to Tom's lips. Not to mention how true the remark actually was. Instead, he kept an impassive face and asked, "Would you be interested in buying 'em?"

The man cleared his throat, rubbed a hand over his shiny pate, and started looking over the weapons, working the action of each a few times. "I don't usually buy second-hand firearms. But since these are in such good condition, yeah, I'll take them."

They dickered over the price a little, the clerk regarding Tom in a quizzical manner the entire while, but the money received for the rifles was fair. And when the transaction was completed, Tom said he would come by early the next morning for a bill of goods, then left before the fellow might ask why he'd been in possession of so many guns.

Over a plate of steak and potatoes in the cafe of the hotel, Cooper's mind wandered to Belle and their future together. He could still feel the warm touch of her lips. Maybe the Landises were back on the east side of the Sabine. Oh, how he hoped so! Now was his chance to settle in a place that felt like home, the first to do that since leaving Ohio four years ago.

A deep pinkish purple glowed behind the buildings on the west side of the street when he came back out on the walk. Darkness would be total in a few minutes, and the town was calm, unlike some of the bigger places he'd been where it became quite boisterous with the setting of the sun. It was very peaceful.

Turning, he walked toward a saloon two buildings down on his left. A drink would be good before going up to his room. As he extended his hand to swing open the batwing doors, he glanced over them at a nearby table and froze.

Ike, James, and Cal were seated there, no more than half a dozen steps away. Tom flattened himself against the outside wall, hoping they hadn't seen him and wondering where the other two were.

Chapter Twelve

Despite the coolness of twilight Tom broke into a sweat. The Landises' mounts were not at the hitch rail. Cooper looked up and down the street and didn't recognize any of the few horses that were standing in front of the stores and homes. That meant the three men's horses were also at the livery, thus, Ike and his brothers were staying in town.

He had nearly bumped right into them. Tom retraced his steps to the hotel and went up to his room. In darkness, he sat on the bed and had a smoke. His enemies were likely going to be spending the night in the same building as himself, and he could barely swallow the idea.

If these three had ridden in for supplies, Bill and Dirk must have stayed close to Stan, Belle, and her parents—where they figured him to be too. Luck had been with him so far, but now the old worry for his friend and future family crept back to mind. What was going on back at the camp? Were they all right?

Tom suddenly wanted to rush to the stables, get his mustang, and head back. But he wouldn't be able to get the things he'd come for until the mercantile opened after daylight, and his bunch would be no better off upon his return than before his departure. Tom rebuked himself for not making the purchases when he sold the rifles. Yet how was he to know of this turn of events?

Standing, Tom dropped the butt of his cigarette into the chamber pot beside the bed. He locked the door and placed the single chair firmly against it for added security. The Colt was in his hand when he stretched out on the feather mattress, and the resolve of being ready to ride when the merchant first opened his store the next morning was settled in his head.

Ike had enjoyed their first night in Maple Springs; it was great to sleep in a bed again. All of them had slept quite late, and other than buying the needed foodstuffs and loading it into their saddlebags at the livery, the day had been spent loafing in the saloon. It was late afternoon when the idleness got to James enough to speak up again.

"We're wasting time and money. We could've been back with Dirk and Bill by now. They're probably in bad shape for grub! Why don't we just head back now?"

"I ain't worried about Bill. He's capable and agrees with what we're doin'," Ike said. "As for Dirk, that boy's been complaining the whole way. If he'll get off his ass and kill some game, they'll make out fine."

The smokey atmosphere of the saloon, though he'd become real accustomed to such places during his life, was beginning to feel stuffy to James. He ignored his glass of whiskey and thought aloud, "I'm worried about that matter at the livery. You're right, there ain't no law, but that hostler ain't too scrawny a fella."

Ike rolled his eyes. "He don't even wear a gun. Just start talkin' to him, and I'll put him in a deep sleep."

"It'll be three against one," Cal added.

No more was said by James. Still, something told him it wasn't a good idea.

Ike bought a quart of whiskey for Bill as they left the saloon. There was just enough funds left to pay for the hotel rooms. He paused to warn James and Cal before entering his own.

"Be up way before daylight so we can get our business done."

Tom bathed at the washstand and donned his new shirt and pants from the store in Bentosa before slipping into his worn duster. With his saddlebags over his shoulder, he adjusted the Colt on his hip, picked up the Spencer, and blew out the lamp before going down to pay for the night's stay.

The air out on the boardwalk was frosty. Lanterns still lighted the way, for it was a half-hour until sunrise. Tom went through an alley and proceeded in the darkness behind the buildings to the livery stables. At the rear of the barn, he stopped at sounds of a scuffle. Light filtered down the adjacent alley and shone on a small door. Tom went to it and heard a dull smack, then something heavy crumpling to the floor. There was a jumble of excited, inaudible voices that diminished with the closing of a door.

After setting the bags down, Tom gripped the carbine and pulled gently on the doorknob, his heart pounding. The door gave and he stepped into a lamp-lit room with his rifle's muzzle ahead of him. Shep Barlow lay sprawled near a cot, his face illuminated ghostly pale, a trickle of blood staining his red hair. Tom knelt and felt a steady pulse, at the same time listening to the bustling activity in the inner part of the barn. His own black was in there with the apparent thieves.

Blowing out the lamp so he wouldn't be silhouetted in the doorway, he waited a moment for his eyes to adjust, then he jerked it open and stepped through. A lantern hung from the wall between him and Ike Landis. The men's gaze held for only a couple of heartbeats before the latter's shout broke the stillness.

"It's Cooper!" His rifle cracked at the exact instant.

The bullet shattered splinters from the doorframe on Tom's right and he unleashed his Spencer as he jumped back behind the wall, knowing it was a miss as he did. He set the Spencer down and drew the .44 because it could be operated quicker in a tight spot. Ike yelled at James to keep him busy, and Tom tried to get the advantage by firing first, but the blast of a shotgun and a sting in his gun arm forced him back after one, wild shot.

Luckily Barlow was far enough over to be shielded by the wall, too, for another charge of buckshot ripped through the door and plastered the floor, desk, and opposite wall. Tom sent three rapid shots in answer, very aware that he might wound his own horse in one of the stalls, and felt his britches jerk above the top of his left boot a fraction of a second before James's revolver barked.

He reached forward and pulled the door shut and stepped aside as two holes were blown through the thin planks. He holstered the Colt, grabbed the Spencer, and eased back outside. The corral was to his left and he ducked between the rails and did the same at the other side. He crouched at the corner of the stables just as one of the Landises swung open the front doors and hurried back inside. Cooper had a clean line of fire down the deserted street and waited. Light had come to life inside some of the businesses and houses, no doubt aroused by the gunfire. But no one was about as of yet. Day was just breaking, and a dog barked somewhere.

"I think I got him!" One of the Landises shouted.

Ike commanded, "C'mon, let's get."

Prancing hooves could be heard a moment, and Tom ran sideways to the middle of the street, vowing to himself that if the Landises planned on riding out the north end of town, they would have to do it over him. Cal led the charge from the livery, with James next, and Ike bringing up the rear with the sorrel mare.

Tom's first shot zipped by the young man's arm, and the roar took them all by surprise.

Tom was aligning his sights on James as he turned to follow Cal south, and Ike grabbed iron and cursed. "Ride, Ride!"

Despite the whistling nearness of Ike's pistol ball, Tom didn't flinch when he squeezed the trigger. James's body was thrown against the saddle horn by the huge slug. Yet he managed to hang on.

The rest of Cooper's shots were deliberately aimed high at Ike's back for fear of hitting the trailing mare. None had an obvious effect on the hunkered rider, and the three soon disappeared into the shadows of the tree-lined road at the end of the street. By that time doors began to slam and several men were approaching. Two in the lead carried rifles, and Cooper waved to them while loading his guns.

"Come on, Barlow's hurt!"

Soon there was a group gathered around Shep, who was beginning to come to on his own. He was still very pale and, in response to the many questions, said, "Feel pretty woozy. One of them fellas just up and slugged me."

"Somebody should get a doctor," Tom advised after telling his own portion of the story.

A middle-aged man ordered a younger, well-dressed gentleman, "Go get old man Frizby." To Tom, he said, "He doctors ever'thing from kids to cows. You could stand to see him, too."

Tom noticed his arm for the first time since the fight. His sleeve was bloody but it hadn't affected the movement of his arm to any great degree, and there would be time to worry about it later. Right now he wanted to be moving, wanted to get back to Belle and the others.

He handed Shep some money where he now lay on the cot. "I'll get the mustang and mule myself. Take care of that head."

Barlow looked at the three twenty-dollar gold pieces and shook his head. "This is too much pay, Cooper."

"Whatever's left over from my bill, let it go on what they stole. I've got a feeling that I may get it back from 'em. Those same fellows have done bad by some other people I know." He went out quickly and saddled the horse and mule, which fortunately were unscathed by the flying lead, retrieved his saddlebags behind the barn, and hurried to the general store. The sun was up now, and he saw a quantity of blood in the street that proved he'd hit James.

The clerk was beyond being curious, he was nosy about the happenings up the way, especially since the blood on Cooper's duster showed he was involved. Tom answered his questions short and frank but offered nothing. It was almost comical the way the bald man scrutinized him over his glasses, however Tom hurried him to fill his order, including dresses for Martha and Belle, and an outfit for Shane. He was disgusted at the damage done to his own new suit, but did not buy another.

To ensure against an ambush Tom rode north, circled, and headed south well away from the traveled route, skirting around an occasional farm, anxious to get back. He told himself that it was only bad timing that brought about the incident, but still he couldn't be sure that the Landises had meant to back off.

Ike Landis knew his brother was hit hard. He flipped the reins of the mare to Cal after they were away from the fight and practically held James in the saddle. They left the road and were going no faster than a trot. Once they almost rode into a farmyard and were forced to make a detour. Blood covered the front of James's clothing, saddle, and the horse's withers. They weren't much more than a mile from town, but Ike called a halt in a secluded spot and ordered Cal to help him get James down so he could examine the wound and maybe stop the bleeding.

Through the pain and weakness James tried to object. "No. We . . . we need to keep . . . goin'. They might—"

His words were cut off with a grunt as they pulled him from the saddle. He couldn't support his own weight and they eased him to the ground. In the early light both could see a wide streak of crimson coming from their brother's mouth.

Cal's voice threatened to crack. "He's gonna be okay?"

His oldest brother didn't answer, but when the wound was exposed Cal had to look away, bile in his throat. Ike had seen such in the war and shook his head. The slug had torn a ragged exit hole in the right side of James's chest and it was amazing that he was even alive. Ike pressed the blood soaked shirt and coat to the gaping wound, knowing there was no way he could hope to stop the steady outward flow of his brother's life.

James tried to speak again and went into a coughing spasm that covered his chin with bloody froth. His hands clutched Ike's jacket as his body trembled. Then he lay still, eyes fixed blankly on the brightening sky.

"He's dead, ain't he?" Cal asked.

Ike nodded, grief and guilt heavy in his throat, while closing James's eyes. His words were very husky. "Don't see how he hung on as long as he did."

"Cooper!" the younger man blurted. "Where'd he come from, anyway?"

"The devil it seems." Ike began wrapping the corpse in its own bedroll. "Ain't no tellin' how close we are from another farm. Let's get him buried." He saw tears wetting his little brother's cheeks and continued, "We'll make that Yankee pay. Choke it down, we got to hurry."

With a knife and tin plates digging an adequate grave was exhausting as well as sad work. It took a long time, and they were alert for anyone hounding their back trail. There was no one, and they worked without talk, their thoughts wild and irrational.

Cal wanted to send the man that had brought so much harm to his family back to the devil with a belly full of lead. There was no doubt that that was where he came from, with a mission to destroy the Landis family. It was hard to believe that Randy and James had been with them a little over a month before, all having a good time at the New Year's party back home.

As Ike's mind began to clear, he worried and dreaded facing Bill and Dirk, the last most of all. He said very little before covering the body in its final resting place. What could he say? He was sorry. Yet, in his dangerously enraged mind, he was already forming a plan to make it up to his two dead siblings.

His arm had long since stopped bleeding by the time he arrived at camp. Nevertheless, Tom was bombarded with questions at the sight of the stains. He explained, assured them that he'd returned with everything he was sent after, and asked if all had been well. It had, absolutely nothing out of the ordinary had taken place, and Shane was inclined to wonder if things might soon be back to normal. Tom advised that they should still take precautions for a few days before really getting to work, and Stan fully agreed. The Peterses were astounded but very grateful that Tom had been thoughtful enough to purchase them clothing after what he'd been through the same morning.

Belle insisted that he sit down and allow her to clean the laceration the buckshot pellet had made above his elbow. The muscle was stiff, and her soft touch was soothing. "You haven't told them?" he asked as she finished with the bandaging.

"No. I was waiting like we decided."

"Then it's time," he asserted, standing and holding her hand. They went over to her parents and the squeeze of her fingers was reassuring.

"Shane, Martha," he said, "there's something we have to tell you. I know I haven't been around long . . . and you have been through a lot because of me. But. . . ." A knowing, pleasant look came to their faces and made it easier for him to finish. "I have fallen in love with your daughter. And she has agreed to marry me once we get things going straight. I realize it doesn't look real promising right now, but I'm sure I can make her a good home. I hope we have your blessings."

Martha smiled and came forward to embrace her daughter. Peters stood from where he sat on a stack of wood. He shook Tom's hand firmly, even more so than on the day they first met, and stated, "When a man gets my age, it's awful nice to know there'll be a good man to take care of his girl after he's gone. Be proud to have you as a son-in-law!"

A solemn day had become almost festive. Stan's hard face softened with a grin as he gripped Tom's shoulder and declared, "I knew there was something between you two."

Tom looked at Belle's radiant smile and nodded at his Indian friend.

Chapter Thirteen

"Where's James?" Dirk demanded with a sick feeling upon seeing his brother's empty, bloodstained saddle.

Ike let Cal take care of the four mounts while he told the horrible details. Bill Landis mumbled to himself and Dirk turned away with clenched fists. The coincidence was unbelievable.

Dirk was mad at everyone, including himself and Cooper. Most of all he was angry with Ike and Randy. Their baby brother had started this all, and Ike, along with more of the family's bloodshed, had finally made him want the Yankee's death too. Was he going insane? No, he was ready for a showdown, but he wanted it soon.

He barked, "Why didn't you come on back after the

first night? Where did the crazy idea of knockin' out the stableman come from?"

"I made that decision!" Ike yelled back. Then he told of wanting some time to pass so Cooper would let down his guard. Next, he related his latest plan for *finishing* it.

Bill and Cal murmured their approval but Dirk sat down, his brow furrowed even more. "I don't like the notion of messing with a woman," he said flatly.

Ike had figured as much from him and shot back, "It'll be the safest and easiest for us! We got plenty of grub, and we'll wait for a good time before we try to take her. If he cares for that girl like you said it appeared, then he'll give himself up for her safety." The big man went to the fire with a bunch of the supplies, his tone became sarcastic. "If I'm feeling generous, I'll let her go."

The fact that two brothers were now dead made Dirk decide not to buck it; also, with a man like Cooper, plus the Indian, they needed to get the upper hand any way they could. However, he vowed not to let Ike hurt the young woman, even if it meant fighting his oldest brother. Therefore, he was glad when Ike said they would be the two—mainly because Dirk was the only one left that knew the camp's location—to stay close and wait for an opportunity.

"Y'all will have to watch out good for that sneaky Indian and that other darn cur they've still got," Bill warned, working his sore shoulder. He was mending quickly and, though respectably wary, aching for vengeance more than ever.

*   *   *

It was the third morning after Cooper's return before he felt it safe enough to begin work on rebuilding the destroyed house. Other than Stan making another trip to his farm to get a few sacks of corn for the animals, they had all hung around the camp most of the time, watching and waiting for more trouble to start. Unexpectedly the days passed in peace, Tom and Belle growing rapidly closer, and everyone had gained new hope.

The Peterses were left with the task of clearing away the rubble of the burnt cabin—the new one was to be erected in the same spot—while Tom and Stan were felling a number of straight pines in a stand of heavy timber near the field. Both men were efficient, but the Caddo was much faster; it had been some time since Tom had swung an ax for anything more than firewood. However, the morning air was quite cool and allowed a man to work with gusto.

Using a rope by tying it to the saddle horn on the buckskin mule and fastening the opposite end to a log, they had dragged a dozen of them up to the building site by noon. Shane hobbled out of the blackened area and told Tom, "Sure picked a fine animal. He'll make good work stock."

"Don't know about a plow yet," Tom said as he slipped the rope from the last log, "but he's good for pullin' these."

Peters mopped his unshaven face with a handkerchief and sat down on one of the logs that would be the foundation for his new home. "We been at it since daylight and, I don't know about y'all, but I could use some dinner. Why don't you fellas help me get the last of this junk outta the way while the women fix a bite? Then we'll get these logs squared up after we eat."

It was agreed, and Stan handed Martha the Sharps carbine and some ammunition for it. She dropped the heavy .56 cartridges into her apron pocket and rode double with Belle on the gray mule's bare back.

The old farmer sent his dog trotting off with them and instantly returned to cleaning up the last of the debris. It was amazing how well he could get around on his sore leg.

Tom enjoyed the work alongside Shane and Stan, who labored as hard as if it had been his own place. It seemed as though things were finally going right.

Dirk was worried upon arriving on their watch of the campsite for the third morning in a row. It was only an hour after dawn, and the little hollow next to the creek was deserted, so they were stationed much closer this time than on their previous vigils. The food supplies that hung in a holly testified that the group wasn't gone for good, though he was still nervous. Two entire days of waiting for a chance, with a couple of close calls at nearly being discovered, was getting to him.

When the two women rode into the opening alone it seemed a blessing to Ike. He readied his legs under him, spurs absent from his boots, and watched. Martha leaned the Sharps, which had once been James's,

against a tree and talked to her daughter while lowering a kettle of beans that hung out of reach of varmints. She placed them to heat over the coals that
Belle was stoking.

The yellow dog began a low, guttural growl as he
sniffed the air, and Ike stepped into view just as Martha went for the Sharps. "I wouldn't do that!" She
halted and stared with horror at the big, untidy man.

Bull suddenly snarled and lunged for the enemy.
Dirk came out of the thicket to the side and dispatched
the dog in midair with a charge of buckshot. Belle
cried out at the blast and sight of her father's dog
being mangled with lead, and Dirk swore as he replaced the shell. He wanted to keep the gun fully
loaded.

Ike levelled his carbine on Martha as he went forward and grabbed Belle. "Get the rifle," he directed
his brother as he backed away with his captive.

"What do you want with her?" Martha almost cried
and came toward them, but she was halted by the wav-
ing of Ike's gun.

"That ain't smart," he declared, steadily retreating
with the helpless girl. "It won't be hard for Cooper to
find our camp if he really wants to. Tell him if he ever
wants to see this pretty little thing alive again he'll
come to us before sundown."

Martha's tears were pouring down her cheeks before
they were even out of hearing with her daughter.

Just a few stunned seconds elapsed between the
time the gunshot reached his ears until Tom had the

black mustang in a dead run back for their camp. Stan
and Shane were no more than three lengths behind him
when he pulled to a sliding stop before Martha. Icy
fingers of fear gripped Tom's throat as he asked the
question, already knowing the sickening answer.

The elderly woman was wringing her hands and
crying as she said, "Two of those men took her. The
big one said to come to their camp before sundown if
you want to see her alive." She sobbed. "Oh, God, I'm
afraid!"

"Which way did they head?" Tom cut in.

As she pointed south he started to wheel his horse,
but Stan grasped the cheek strap of its bridle. "Wait!
They'll be waiting for you."

Tom's veins were afire. "I've got to get to them by
sunset! You heard what she said!"

"Yes, but there is plenty of light. Let me find 'em
and see what's the best way to get at them. If you just
ride in, they'll shoot you down, and there would still
be no guarantee of ever gettin' Belle back."

Like always, the Indian's words were simple and
true, and Tom took a deep breath. He heard Shane
curse for the first time, at having allowed his wife and
daughter to go off alone, but the old man added, "He's
right, Tom. They're a-wantin' you to go off half-
cocked. Stan is the best one to slip around and find
their weaknesses before we try somethin'."

Tom nodded consent and the Caddo slipped from
the dun's back and went into the brush on silent, moc-
casined feet. Cooper tied the mounts with the gray
mule, while Shane tried to console his wife, then

paced with a cigarette. It was all too clear that the Landises had just been watching and waiting for a chance.

The fear that he felt for his future wife was nearly unbearable. What was she going through at this moment? He sat down at the base of a sweet gum and clenched his eyes at the thought.

If I can just get her back. . . . If I'm ever going to have a normal life with her, he concluded, *I have to end it now.*

The threesome were tortured with terrible thoughts for three hours before Stan Waters came striding back into camp. "I found them," he answered their questioning eyes. "At least three miles southwest of here. Tom, the one you shot must've died. There were only four."

Cooper crushed yet another smoke under his boot heel. He doubted nothing his Caddo friend said, but couldn't help but be amazed at the speed in which he'd traveled the distance on foot. "All right, we need to move. Shane, you and Martha move our camp across the creek and get a good spot. This isn't a safe place as long as they know where it's situated.

"We might have to ride hard and we'll come right back through here. If you can, leave Martha hid there and get positioned in a defensive place between here and where you set up the camp. Stan can drop off with you and hold off the Landises—if they're following— until I can leave Belle with Martha and get back." His words were confident, more so than he felt. As for the plan of actually getting her away from her captors, it remained undeveloped.

"I'll do it. Y'all be careful." Peters began to load the gear on the two mules with his wife's help. Stan mounted his dun and told Tom to follow, then comforted them all with the words, "She was unharmed while I was there. And I got close."

The Caddo rode swiftly through the timber, as if he'd made the trip a hundred times, until crossing the wagon road. Not much further he stopped and explained that they must continue without the horses. Cooper unbuckled his spurs and left them in his saddlebags.

His mind whirled for a strategy, knowing all too well that a simple rush could likely end with everyone, even Belle, lying dead. "How much further?" he whispered. "Guards?"

"Little over two hundred yards. Bill, the man I wounded the other day, is between us," Stan said and moved on with a nocked arrow. Tom followed with the Spencer, his every step a strain for silence as he scanned the surroundings. Sundown wasn't far off, maybe an hour. There was no defined trail; tall trees and chaparral closed in on every side.

Bill Landis could finally be discerned crouched beneath a magnolia thirty steps ahead. His left side was to them and he wasn't aware of their presence. Cooper stopped Stan as he began to draw back the bowstring.

"If we can take him alive, we could use him for a trade."

Stan eased the tension off the bow and dipped his

chin. "Stay here. Move in when I signal." Before waiting on a reply he began to circle so as to approach the sentry from behind.

Tom squatted and watched his stealthy companion with held breath. There was a time when the buckskin-clad figure couldn't be seen, each second endless, but suddenly his form materialized like a specter at the rear of the guard. Bill flinched but made no sound as the Colt Dragoon was stuck into his back. Stan relieved him of the Sharps and waved Tom in.

Hurrying up, Tom took his six-gun, shoved it in his waistband, and murmured, "Don't try to give a warning, just walk right into your camp." Landis started to mouth a reply and Tom pressed the muzzle of his carbine into the man's stomach. "Or you can die right here."

Bill turned and marched toward the little opening in the midst of a stand of pines. "That you, Bill?" Dirk challenged just before they appeared.

"What the—" Ike rose from a stump near Belle on the ground, but he was halted from raising his breech-loading rifle by the click of the Sharps in Stan's hands.

"None of you move," Tom directed. "I'll cut him in half."

Bill liked the fact not a bit that his own body was shielding Cooper. The look of Ike was dangerous. "Darned Indian walks like a cat!" Bill exclaimed in his own defense.

By holding tightly to the back of Bill's collar, Tom controlled the man's movements with tugs and prods of the .56 carbine. His voice rose sternly. "Move away from her, Ike! She's coming with us unless you don't care if Bill sees nightfall!"

That now familiar cloud started to settle over Ike's mind, and he tried to fight it back. He was careful not to move his downward pointing rifle, but said, "What's to say we don't shoot her down right now?"

There was no sign that Belle had been handled roughly, and Tom was grateful, but her eyes were full of tears. "Uh-uh," he said, voice hard, the same as it was that day in Bentosa, Bill noticed. "Stan will have you spitting blood first. By that time I'd have Bill laid out and be working on the other two."

The words were true, and it set a fiery rage in Ike's soul. The Indian was less than twelve feet away, the Sharps trained at his broad chest. Dirk had his hand on the butt of his revolver, yet it was a genuine fact that he wouldn't do harm to the girl. He was in the wrong position even if he tried, for Ike was between the two. And Cal was caught in an awkward position as he reached for the shotgun. Ike had been so sure, and now his plans were undermined again by this damned Yankee and Indian.

"All right," he remarked slowly, letting his long gun fall. "But you can bet this ain't the end of this. You're gonna pay for my two brothers' deaths!"

Belle walked quickly over to Tom, careful not to step between the two factions. Her ears were attuned to Tom's rough voice, rougher than she ever believed possible from him.

"I didn't figure it would be," he said. "Tomorrow

I'll be back! You want me dead, so you'll have your chance. . . . In a fair fight."

"And how can we be sure you won't skin out while we're waitin' on you?" Cal inquired, wondering if he should make a play. However, Cooper's even harder tone put all heroic thoughts aside.

"I will not run anymore. I'll be here at dawn!" Without diverting his glance from the enemy, he directed Stan, "Get Belle to the horses."

Stan disappeared instantly with the young woman, and Tom began backing away and pulling Bill with him. "He's gonna be our insurance. He'll be left all right as long as you don't try to follow us to the horses. Otherwise, you'll find out."

Ike, Dirk, and Cal watched in anger as Tom and Bill went out of sight. The Caddo was aboard the dun and Belle in Tom's saddle when he prodded Bill to a halt. Sheathing the Spencer, Tom swung up behind the woman's attractive figure and looked down at the scarred Landis face. "Pride's killed lots of men. If you've got more sense than the rest, you'll be on your way back to Louisiana tonight."

Bill's fury was evident in the sound of his words. "I'll see your blood *first*."

Cooper's left hand was in front of Belle gripping the reins, the other touching the handle of his Colt. There was no use in saying anything further, all was set, and he sent the black galloping away ahead of Stan. The speed at which they traveled didn't allow conversation and they soon splashed across the creek and saw Shane with his rifle behind a cluster of willows. Stan gave Tom his reins and glided from his mustang's back to land near the farmer without slowing their pace. Cooper continued in the direction Peters motioned.

The new encampment was a couple of hundred yards from the creek, beyond a depression and thick strip of cane in which Tom deposited the dun, where Shane had left his saddled mule. Martha Peters hugged her daughter and voiced a prayer of thanks after she swung down. Cooper shucked the carbine and handed it to Belle.

"If you hear gunshots, hide." He started back, left his horse with Stan and Shane's mounts, and proceeded to the men's side on foot.

"No sign of 'em, yet," Shane whispered in the cold light of dusk when Tom squatted between them.

Stan said, "I don't think they'll show. Probably play it safe and wait for us tomorrow."

Tom shook his head as he gazed across the waterway. "I don't aim to implicate you any more, Stan. I'll go alone."

Peters grimaced and rubbed his stiff growth of beard. "Stan told me about that. You really gonna do it, Son?"

"I have to get this over." He looked down, worried. "I love your daughter with all my heart, and I can't offer her a good life if we're always havin' to run. I'd rather die trying to prevent that."

"I hate it, but I understand," the old man asserted. "If I wasn't afraid to leave the women alone, I'd want to be in this fight with you." There was a short time where nothing but the forest's sounds were audible. "I can't thank you two enough for gettin' my girl back. They didn't hurt her, did they?"

The shake of Cooper's head was barely discernable. "She seemed fine. But I haven't been able to talk with her."

"I *will* be with you," Stan stated sternly.

It was fully dark now, and only a tiny strip of moon and starlight illuminated the Indian's stoic features. "Stan, I don't expect that of you. Shane is still going to need a lot of help if I die."

"Four against one is not good. This way, there will be two of them apiece. And you're forgetting that I owe you."

In the dark Tom could feel, more than see, the friendly presence of his two older companions. "How does your father's people say 'friend' again?" he asked Stan.

"*Taysha.* Some white men say it's where Texas got its name."

Tom Cooper laid a hand on both men's shoulders before standing. "That's all I've found in Texas. Without you two I wouldn't have made it this long."

"In spite of it all, I'm sure glad you passed our way," Peters said and got up. "A man can't ever have enough friends.

"C'mon, those varmints ain't gonna do nothin' but let you come to them. And I want to see how Belle is doin'."

During the ride back to the women Cooper continuously flexed his right arm. It was sore and stiff from the buckshot wound and his labor with the ax, and he knew it could effect his draw. That was more than enough to cause concern.

Chapter Fourteen

Shane Peters questioned his daughter about her treatment in the Landis camp while Stan built a fire for warmth and light. Tom stood next to Belle and listened as she said, "They didn't harm me, just scared me with some of the things the big one said about Tom. They're so horrible!" She clung to Cooper and told her father of how Bull had tried to protect them.

Shane nodded and concluded, "He and Jack were both mighty good dogs."

Martha began to warm the beans in the kettle as her husband took over for Stan at building up a good cooking fire. The Caddo, fully armed, came up to Tom and announced, "I'm gonna make a round or two while supper's being fixed. We can plan out tomorrow after we eat."

166

Belle looked at Tom when Stan had departed, suspicion in her face. "What are y'all going . . ." Then she knew, and her beautiful eyes grew wide. She'd been troubled over it the whole time. "I thought, hoped, that you only told them that so we could get away without a fight! Oh, Tom, you can't face them again. Please don't, it would be too dangerous even with Stan."

Tom held her gently at the edge of the camp away from her parents. "I have to, honey. I don't want to live another day being afraid to let you out of my sight. I promise not to do anything foolish." He saw tears well up and spill from her eyes, and he wished he could say something more to reassure her, but he would not make any more promises that he might not be able to keep, for he knew full well the chances one sometimes has to take to win a fight. And he was quite sure this one would be to the death.

She looked down at the bullet holes in his clothing and touched his arm lightly. "This whole thing is foolish. And they've come so close to getting what they want."

Tom thought of the uselessness of more bloodshed and agreed, "I know. But there's no other way to stop it. Just remember, that whatever happens, I love you."

Laying her head against his chest and hugging him tightly, she said, "I love you, too. . . . Be careful."

He vowed he would try and held her for several minutes while she cried softly. As he stood there he thought of the very real possibility that he would never get to live a life with this woman who he truly loved.

That was what worried him more than death itself. He kissed her after she managed to compose herself, and they joined her mother and father by the fire.

The evening meal was a very solemn occasion and Tom and Stan were the first to finish. They moved into some deep shadows and began a thorough discussion of the next morning. It was obvious, since the Landises knew they were coming, that they would be more cautious. They decided to be on the move well before dawn, so they would have time to approach the campsite in darkness. Also, considering the odds, Stan recommended a crossfire, and Tom agreed. For a time the two talked of precise actions.

"Got plenty of ammunition," Tom said with a grin as he inhaled a cigarette to life.

Stan grunted with mirth. "I got all of that box of .56's you bought for my Sharps, the five loads left in this"—he touched the Dragoon at his waist—"and a dozen arrows. If we do it like we plan, there won't be a need for even half."

Tom chuckled, hoping things *would* go as they had discussed, and the two settled into a lengthy span of quiet pondering. Finally, Stan said, "I do have one favor to ask you."

"Anything. What is it?"

"I have lived like the white man, but when I die, I want to be buried the Caddoan way."

The word "when" bothered Tom greatly. Did his friend have a premonition? He'd heard of such things happening, and it sobered his mood much more. Yet he didn't change expressions when he said, "Tell me how."

Stan took a deep breath and returned as calmly as ever, "The grave is dug immediately and the body placed in it with the head to the west. Food is placed in the grave, too, along with some personal articles, like my weapons, for use in the next life."

"If it comes to that, I'll see to it personally. Unless I'm dead too." Cooper finished his smoke and stubbed it out. "And if it should be the other way around, you make sure I'm planted with my boots and gunbelt on. That's how I've lived for the majority of my life, and I might as well meet my Maker that way."

Stan's thin smile and nod showed that the wish would be carried out. "I'll take the first watch." He rose and strode away before Tom could say another word.

Bill returned to the camp after Cooper had made good their escape, and he found Ike pacing and swearing in a tight circle, his carbine held in a death grip. The other two were sitting quietly by a little fire, and Bill, now having no weapon, picked up the scattergun. He checked the twin loads of buckshot, then hunkered near Cal and said nothing.

Fury choked Ike's voice when he spoke. "If that man don't show, I'll keep on till I kill every darned one of that farmer's bunch too!"

Dirk was checking each chamber in the cylinder of his revolver and making sure of the smoothness of its action as he said, "Oh, he'll show." He wasn't thrilled over the fact, but his nerves had begun to still themselves automatically, like they always did before an upcoming fight, and his cool tone stopped his oldest brother's futile walking. "You could see it in his eyes," Dirk explained. "We've pushed him as far as he's gonna be pushed. There'll be a battle tomorrow."

Ike Landis had noted himself the look of the Northerner and tried to hide his own uneasiness by commenting sarcastically, "I'm surprised you ain't whining for the lot of us to head home."

Dirk slipped the gun back in the holster and reclined against his saddle. He couldn't and did not try to hide his bitterness. "I told you I'd stick. This is what we've been after—a chance to drop that murdering Yankee. Just relax and wait on him."

Bill heard Ike mumble something but was too preoccupied with his own thoughts to know what it was. The Indian had made a fool of him, and, though the feeling of danger was making a heavy presence, he wanted the red man's blood almost as bad as he did Cooper's. "That Indian will be with him."

"Let 'em come," Cal blustered. It was finally coming to a showdown and he was excited with the urge of vengeance.

Ike Landis began to calm, his mind clearing enough to think. "Let that fire start to die a little after midnight," he ordered Cal. There would be no sleep tonight; he wanted to think some more.

Tom had been awake for over three hours with his turn at guard duty. During that time he had exercised his gun arm. It was still two hours to daylight, but everyone in camp was stirring. By the light of the fire, Tom and Stan were making preparations to leave. The mustangs, sensing the time to be moving, made eager noises and motions.

Hating that Belle was seeing him do it, Tom tied the Colt down low with a leather thong. He tucked the pistol that was taken from Bill in his waistband at his back. Its barrel was considerably shorter than his Army Model, and the gun was concealed from view by the duster, thus making it a good hideout weapon.

Belle was fighting hard to keep the tears back. She came to him before he mounted and declared, "I wish this wasn't happening."

Cooper touched the softness of her chin and brought her wet eyes to meet his stare. "Me too. Now remember what I said last night." She nodded, and he kissed her lightly before turning to mount the black.

Shane walked up with his wife and put an arm around Belle's shoulders. "I wish I could stand with you two against those devils," he said woefully. "Y'all both remember, a man ain't no less for retreatin' from a fight he ain't winnin'."

Stan and Tom dipped their chins, yet both knew there would be no retreating on their part. And if the opposing faction did, they would have to be hasty, for Cooper and the Caddo meant to end this darn feud.

Belle looked at Stan. "Thank you for goin' with him. Watch yourself."

The Indian's face creased in a smile. "I owe him. And besides, I want to see you two married."

Then they were gone. Martha clenched her daughter's hand and said a prayer. At the same time, Tom was hoping that he hadn't touched Belle's beauty for the last time.

The starlight was dim and their progress slow, but Stan led the way steadily once again, as if his eyes could penetrate the darkness. Maybe they could. Anyhow, just a short time passed before he halted to let the black move alongside his dun.

He leaned over and whispered in Tom's ear, "We're a little ways south of where we left the horses last night."

Stepping down, each knew what to do. A thin line of gray was appearing in the east as they eased through brush and vines that threatened to trip them or warn of their approach. So his fingers would be free, Cooper had removed his gloves, and now the cold made them somewhat numb. Surprisingly no guard shouted an alarm or fired upon them, and they stopped and knelt when the glowing red coals of a dying fire came in sight.

"Funny there hasn't been an incident yet," Tom remarked.

Stan touched his arm. "I'm gonna get in position before better light. I'll let you start it." He moved off to the left, his movements almost as quiet as a shadow, and Tom was left to await sunup alone.

Chapter Fifteen

A ghostly, foreboding fog shrouded the edges of the clearing, which was first to become visible. Tom Cooper licked his dry lips. The circled form of beds lay motionless, and looked suspicious. He glanced over his shoulder and saw nothing in the dark thicket of pine saplings. The Landises wouldn't just be lying in the open, and that worried him.

Enough light for shooting finally came, and he gazed at the blankets. A horse snorted across the clearing to the right. Tom smirked—it was a trap, a ploy to draw him into the open. Time to do it, he told himself, stood, and went forward, toward the layer of fog.

"Meet me in the open if we're gonna do this! I ain't gonna run around in the brush!" His words cut the stillness like a warm knife through butter. A muffled curse drifted to him, and then they were marching to meet each other.

The Landis men were coming on abreast, several steps between each, Bill on the left, Cal next, then Ike and Dirk. Cal was the only one who had dozed, his face was bright and his body alive with a mixture of fear and hate. The others' faces were sternly set. Tom halted when they did; some twenty feet stretched between them. His Spencer was pointed down, but it could be brought on target with a flick of the wrist.

"Where's that Indian friend of yours?" Bill demanded.

Stan Waters appeared from the timber at their right flank and said evenly, "Right here."

That started it. Bill wheeled and Stan shot him through the guts. The Caddo discarded the Sharps as a single charge of buckshot plowed the dirt in front of him. Bill was in a seated position, his head sagged, the shotgun dropped to his lap, and Stan was swinging his bow into action against the others.

A ball from Tom's Spencer shattered the stock of Ike's rifle as Bill went down, numbing the big man's hands and staggering him. Dirk Landis made the quickest draw Tom had ever seen, and he felt the burn of the pistol's bullet on his neck. He levered his repeater and shot the man beneath his lower right rib. Dirk stumbled and slumped to his hands and knees. Cooper turned to Cal, expecting the impact of one of the youth's bullets, yet his gun had barely cleared leather. His eyes were glazing and a sob came from his throat as he fell on his face. An arrow was imbedded between his shoulders.

Ike backpedalled five steps before he grabbed iron. Tom was just pivoting the carbine back toward him when the revolver belched flame. He felt a tremendous shock in his left shoulder and the Spencer fired into the ground before he dropped it. He saw the big man crawfishing and cocking the weapon again, and Tom reached for his own belt gun, throwing himself to the side. The enemy's slug hissed by and he hit the ground rolling and shooting from a prone position.

As Stan aimed at the fleeing Ike Landis, Bill, braced on his elbow, managed to unleash the second shot in the scattergun at the hated Indian. One of the pellets grazed Stan's left leg and two dug into his left side. He stumbled, his projectile missing Ike by a three-foot margin, but he kept from going to the earth. Ignoring the pain and whistling nearness of a shot Ike threw at him, Stan nocked another arrow for Bill.

A pool of blood had formed on the ground beside him. He was fumbling weakly to open the shotgun's breech and replace the spent shells. He jerked upright at the bite of the arrowhead into his body and a gurgle issued from his lips as he sprawled his full length.

The leader of the Landis clan was ten feet from the tree line and horses beyond when Tom drew blood. It was his third attempt and only made an insignificant scratch on the forearm of Ike's gun hand, yet it was enough to throw the last shot from his six-gun off target. The bullet hit the ground inches from Tom's face and blinded him with dirt. He heard the twang of

Stan's bowstring, the cursing of Ike as he ran to safety,
and the very near bark of a revolver.

Through burning and watering eyes Tom saw Dirk
straining to back the hammer of his six-shooter again.
Tom rolled on his side and triggered a shot at the man.
When he came to his own knees and turned his attention back to Ike, the big man was gone. The corpse-
strewn clearing was suddenly silent, a haze of
gunsmoke mixed with the fog in the early-morning air.
Then a horse whinnied, started to run in the distance,
and Stan was beside him.

"We gotta get to Shane and the women. Make sure
they're safe." The pain in Tom's bleeding shoulder as
he stood made his words short. He saw Stan's nod of
agreement, but also that his friend had his hand on a
small bloodstain on his left side, and he queried, "How
bad you hit?"

The Caddo jogged with him toward their mounts.
"It's nothing. A couple pellets. You?"

Though Tom's wound was bleeding a good bit, he
explained that no bones felt broken. However, he was
concerned over Stan nearly as much as the Peterses,
but he said nothing more. There was no telling what
Ike Landis's mind might have in store, and he knew
that buckshot wounds were prone to bleed internally.
These things smothered his thoughts as he crashed the
black gelding headlong through the brush. Guiding the
animal with his legs, he was able to get fresh rounds
into his Colt. Thank God he still had full use of his
right arm.

*   *   *

Ike's entire family had been cut down in front of him like so many slaughtered hogs. The dark cloud of fury had enveloped his brain completely, and his thoughts were those of a madman. Getting away wasn't his intention for running. There was no going back to Louisiana for him—not now, without the others. No, he felt certain he would die at the hands of the Yankee, but he was bent on doing one thing first: kill the farmer and his family! If he couldn't get Cooper, he could at least make the man know sorrow.

Landis jerked the sorrel mare to a stop in the center of the campsite where he and Dirk had kidnapped Belle. It was abandoned, nothing in sight. Except distinct tracks. He grunted to himself, gripped his revolver tightly, and spurred toward the creek.

If they were going to move camp, they shouldn't have left such a good trail.

Tom and Stan burst through the cane and into camp without knowing what they were about to see. Fear hit the former like a hammer. Shane, Martha, and Belle were seated in a row on a short piece of log that Stan had dragged up for firewood the night before. Ike, brandishing his pistol with a crazed appearance, stood in front of them. Cooper's hand started to dip for the Colt, but he stopped.

Landis's gun levelled on Belle, his eyes wicked on Tom and the Indian. "Drop your weapons and get down!"

There was no choice in the matter, and Tom's gaze flickered to Stan as he let his gunbelt fall to the mustang's feet. He stepped down then, feeling only a little better at the presence of the pistol against his back, while Stan slowly discarded his armament. The Dragoon was the last to go, and it struck the ground with a thud.

"Both of you come over here. I want you to have a good look at what's fixin' to take place."

About ten feet separated Tom and Stan, and they started forward at the same time. Maybe they could get close enough to try something, if Ike would just avert his gun from the Peterses. But Tom didn't believe he was quick enough for the play, not with his stiff arm.

His speech slurred by anger, Landis halted them twelve paces away. "You ain't got nothin' I want to trade for now! All my family is lyin' back there dead because of you! Now you're gonna wish you'd never come south."

Martha cried out when he pointed the gun at her daughter, and Peters beseeched, "Shoot me, don't hurt the women."

"Shut up old man! I'll get to you, but you're all gonna die for helpin' this darned Yankee!"

Tom thought he saw Stan inch a step closer, and he thought of reaching for the hideout gun while Ike paused, but the big man's gun never wavered from Belle. Maybe there was a way to draw the weapon onto himself so he could try. Tears flowed down Belle's smooth cheeks, and she shrank back as Landis touched the hammer.

"You're the lowest kind of varmint," Tom suddenly

exclaimed, and Ike's eyes centered on him. "You'd kill a woman before a man! You're too darned yellow to stand and fight! You even ran while the rest of your family was bleedin' in the dirt. You know what the Army does with cowards." He could see the rage growing in the man as he went on, "Your whole bunch wasn't nothing but a lot of ignorant, prideful, varmints who didn't know when they were whipped. They—"

Tom cut off short and waved the duster back to get the pistol as Ike cursed him profanely and brought his weapon to bear on him. His movement seemed deathly slow, and he heard the snick of the enemy's six-gun going to full cock, and a shriek from Belle as she and her parents jumped to their feet, his own gun not yet in line. But the slug he was braced for never came.

A shattering war cry came from the Caddo and something sparkled in the early-morning sun. Landis whirled and felled the Indian with a quick shot, but his left hand was already clutching the handle of a knife that was buried to the haft in his breast. Then the Yankee's fist was sending a stream of lead into him from a gun that appeared from beneath the bloody duster. Ike staggered back under the repeated shocks, no longer able to hold his pistol. He fought to keep from falling, but everything turned black and he forgot all the hate.

Tom Cooper stopped working the gun's action when it clicked empty. He watched the man try to walk and crumple. The mounts had loped off a distance in fright. He dropped the revolver and went to his fallen companion, all at once very weak and ill.

A dark spot was spreading amazingly fast around a hole in the middle of the Indian's buckskin shirt and jacket, yet his eyes were open and looking into Tom's face as he knelt beside him.

"I knew we'd . . . do it," he said.

Tom realized that his friend was dying, and tears threatened to spill from his eyes. "You saved our lives. I couldn't have done it if you hadn't drawn him off me. I'm sorry."

"Don't be. Is good thing . . . to die for *tayshas*. Keep the dun. Get anything from my place . . . that'll help out. Stay there if you want. Take . . . good care . . . of Belle."

Stan's chest became still, and Tom watched feebly as the soul departed from the man, a faint smile left on his lips. The others were grouped around. Shane's eyes were deep pools of sadness, and Martha and Belle were crying softly.

"I've known him ever since I was a little girl," the latter murmured.

Her father added, "He was as brave and good as men come—of any color."

"He told me last night, that if this should happen, to bury him the way of the Caddoes," Tom said, standing. Dizziness almost overcame him, and he stepped backwards to regain his balance.

Belle rushed to his side and admonished, "You must be tended to first. God, you've lost a lot of blood!"

"She's right, Son," Peters agreed. "You let Belle take care of those wounds while I ride to the shed and get a couple shovels. I know Stan wouldn't want you bleedin' down."

The last thing he wanted was to sit still, because his mind was replaying the past events in rapid succession. And he wanted to keep his promise to Stan as quickly as possible. However, he allowed Belle to administer to the holes in his shoulder and burn on his neck. He drank a cup of lukewarm coffee with the other hand and talked to them about the method of the Indian burial before Peters went to appropriate the tools.

It would have taken Tom forever to dig the grave alone in his weakened condition. But with the alternate help of Shane and the women, it went quickly. Afterwards, as they readied Stan's body, Tom wondered where the life-saving knife had been concealed and questioned Shane.

"I don't rightly know," the farmer replied. "He always used a short, thin one for dressing animals. Long as I've been around him, I never even knew he carried it. But I think I glimpsed him reachin' over his shoulder right before it all happened."

Kneeling, Tom indeed found a sheath between Stan's shoulders, hidden by his jacket. After retrieving the weapon from Landis's stiffening body, he hefted its wait and balance. The knife was homemade, its handle of bone, and was perfect for throwing. He slid it back into the sheath and sent up a silent prayer of thanks that his friend had been in possession of it. The end of the handle, the one part that wasn't concealed by the buckskins, was completely covered by his long, black hair, shiny even in death.

No one spoke as the corpse, a good portion of jerked venison, and Stan's weapons were lowered into the earth. While Shane and Martha finished filling the grave, Cooper began to carve a few words on a slab of cypress that Peters had also acquired from the smokehouse shed. He felt that everything had been said before his friend passed away, yet he wanted this done.

Belle stayed near him, but allowed him to mourn the loss in quiet, no matter how badly she wanted to embrace and talk with him. Some people needed to be left alone at a time like this. Tom finished, scrutinized his work, and smiled weakly at her before placing the marker at the head of Stan's final resting place, beneath the boughs of a towering pin oak.

The four of them stood for a time in the wintery, midday sun beside the mound of dirt and looked at the epitaph. It read:

STAN WATERS

GRAY HAWK

DIED WITH HONOR 1870

A FINE *TAYSHA*

"That's right nice, Tom," Peters said after explaining the meaning of the last word to the women. "Stan would like that."

Martha's voice was firm and clear, no longer quaking. "To live in the hearts of friends forever, is never to die."

Cooper ducked his head in concurrence as they walked back to the main part of the camp. His shoulder was aching, and he let Belle check it again. As she did he reflected that the Indian would be with them all. Shane gathered the strayed horses. They ate a bit of corn bread and bacon while resting, and then, leading the mare, Tom went over to the grizzly body of Ike Landis.

"Shane, can you help me get him across the horse? I want to bury him with the rest of his family where they fell."

The old farmer stood, leg stiff but very capable of withstanding his weight, and did as requested. Boarding the buckskin mule, he motioned for his wife to hand up the shovels. "We'll be awhile, I'm gonna help him. Everybody should have a decent burial. Y'all have more grub ready when we return. It'll be dark before we get there, but we'll stay at Stan's place tonight."

Before stepping into the leather, Tom put his arm around Belle, but his words were for them all. "Stan gave his life for us, and we can't disappoint him. With some time, the money we get for the Landises' horses and gear, and a lot of hard work, we'll make it." He smiled and kissed Belle on the cheek. "There'll be two cabins to build, but first we've got to go before a preacher. Then we can see how good a farmer Shane can make of me."

Belle watched him ride away with her father, the

sorrel trailing behind with the corpse lashed in place. In spite of the sadness that filled her heart for Stan, she was relieved that she still had this man that she loved. And the future truly appeared promising.